LONE RUNNER

Dirk McLean

D0886025

James Lorimer & Company Ltd., Publishers
Toronto

James Lorimer & Company Ltd., Publishers acknowledges funding support from the Ontario Arts Council (OAC), an agency of the Government of Ontario. We acknowledge the support of the Canada Council for the Arts, which last year invested $153 million to bring the arts to Canadians throughout the country. This project has been made possible in part by the Government of Canada and with the support of Ontario Creates.

Cover design: Tyler Cleroux
Cover image: Shutterstock

9781459415942
eBook also available 9781459415935

Cataloguing data for the hardcover edition is available from Library and Archives Canada.

Library and Archives Canada Cataloguing in Publication (Paperback)

Title: Lone runner / Dirk McLean.
Names: McLean, Dirk, 1956- author.
Series: Sports stories.
Description: Series statement: Sports stories
Identifiers: Canadiana (print) 20200356410 | Canadiana (ebook) 20200356429
    | ISBN 9781459415928 (softcover) | ISBN 9781459415935 (EPUB)
Classification: LCC PS8575.L43 L66 2021 | DDC jC813/.54—dc23

Published by:
James Lorimer &
Company Ltd., Publishers
117 Peter Street, Suite 304
Toronto, ON, Canada
M5V 0M3
www.lorimer.ca

Distributed in Canada by:
Formac Lorimer Books
5502 Atlantic Street
Halifax, NS, Canada
B3H 1G4

Distributed in the US by:
Lerner Publisher Services
241 1st Ave. N.
Minneapolis, MN, USA
55401
www.lernerbooks.com

Printed and bound in Canada.
Manufactured by Friesens in Altona, MB in January 2021.
Job #272147

For Renée, Jessica, Melissa and Ashley
And my mother, Jacqueline
Welcome . . . Chloe

*"Nothing in my life happens in halves.
There was a time when nothing on
my list had changed, now suddenly . . ."*
Harriet's Daughter *by Marlene Nourbese Philip*

*"I am Mokgadi Caster Semenya.
I am a woman and I am fast."*
Olympic middle-distance champion Mokgadi Semenya

Contents

1 Wilderness RACE

"What's your name?"

Michaela wasn't sure if the voice was directed to her. She turned around on the slab of Canadian Shield rock. Water lapped over her feet.

Two white girls stood in front of her. She wondered where the other girl was, the one they were always with. Michaela had overheard that they called themselves the Three Musketeers. They each lived on acres of land with big houses.

"Michaela. Michaela Robinson," she said. *I'm surprised they want to talk to me*, she thought.

Back in March, Mom had taken her to an information session for first-time campers. "Imagine how good it will be for you, child, to experience more of the province. You can't spend another summer just in the city."

"Two whole weeks with the apartment to ourselves," Dad had said. "We'll parade around naked if we feel like it, eh Lorna?" he had joked to Michaela's mom.

Michaela had been at Camp Stone Hearth on Lake

Simcoe for almost the whole two weeks. In all that time, she had not made any friends.

"I'm Bethany," said the girl who had spoken. She twisted her blonde ponytail.

"And I'm Cindy," the short brunette said.

"You looked pretty good in the kayak yesterday," Bethany said. "Your first time?"

Michaela nodded. "I was a little nervous."

"Couldn't tell," Cindy said. She put a piece of chewing gum in her mouth. "Considering you live in the city," she mumbled around the gum.

Three Black girls passed by, laughing among themselves. They were the only girls of colour at the camp, apart from Michaela. She had tried to talk to them when she arrived. But soon she had realized that they had their own high-class clique. There was no room for another "sista."

"You look like a runner, though," Bethany giggled.

"I ran the 400 at Finals," Michaela offered.

"Sprinter. Told you so." Cindy shoved Bethany playfully.

"Come with us," Bethany ordered. "Someone wants to meet you."

Michaela was feeling lost and alone at the camp. There were no girls there from her part of Toronto. There were no girls who had been friendly until now. She would be glad for some company. So she followed Bethany and Cindy.

The third girl was waiting outside a cabin. "That's Rachel," Cindy told Michaela as Bethany whispered into Rachel's ear.

"Did you win at your City Finals?" Rachel asked Michaela. She was as tall and long-legged as Michaela.

"I did okay," Michaela shrugged.

"What's . . . okay?" Rachel prodded.

"Bronze."

"Yeah. That's okay." Rachel smiled. "I'm looking for a fourth for the annual under-14 cross-country race tomorrow."

"We've been coming to this camp since we were seven," Bethany said.

"And we've trained for this race, like, a lot," Cindy added.

"Yep. Rachel even ran alongside us while we were on horseback," Bethany giggled.

Michaela looked at their sporty outfits. High designer logos sparkled in the sunlight. Who needed that kind of thing for camp? She wondered if they had arrived with six suitcases each.

"We really, really wanna win," Rachel stated. "You interested?"

"I've never run cross-country before," Michaela replied. "I was thinking I'd do it this fall."

"You're a runner, aren't you? It's only two kilometres. That's settled then," Rachel said with finality.

Michaela did not want to seem like a spoilsport. She nodded.

Sure, she thought. *I could be the fourth musketeer.*

★★★

Tap, tap. Tap, tap. Tap, tap. Tap, tap.

It was the sound of running shoes upon a dirt track. Now and then twigs cracked.

Huh! Huh! Huh! Huh! Huh! Huh! Huh . . .

Michaela was speeding along with other thirteen-year-old girls. Rachel was in the lead. Michaela figured they had been running for about a minute through the forest.

Before the race they had all been given the important information. There were "2-K" signs taped to trees every two kilometres, with arrows giving directions. For safety, there was a Lead Senior running at the front of the pack and a Rear Senior behind the last runner. Dotted along the way were other Senior Race Assistants in pairs. They held whistles and cell phones, in case a runner fell and injured herself or fainted from the heat.

It was day twelve of camp. *Two more to go*, she thought. Michaela thought about what she liked about being at camp. She had been enjoying the fresher air. She had fallen asleep to the sounds of crickets and other creatures. She enjoyed the songs at mealtimes and had no complaints about the food. She had even tried new activities. But it was almost like she was at camp alone. She hadn't made any friends.

The track opened out to a small clearing. Above, the blistering July sun beat down upon them. She squinted from the glare of the light.

There were four teams of four runners each. All wore white T-shirts and shorts. Michaela and her team had pink ribbons pinned to their left sleeves. The other teams wore red, green and blue ribbons.

They ran along the lake on firm sand. Then they returned to the forested area. The course narrowed to single file. Michaela began to feel her calves on fire.

Maybe I should stop and rest, she thought for the first time.

But there was no place to stop. They were bunched up. It was not the heat that began to affect her. It was the pace. And it was punishing.

No one had given her advice about this type of running. Now she wished she had asked, instead of just jumping in.

Several runners passed Michaela on a country road, including her teammates Bethany and Cindy. Moments later, Michaela looked behind and realized that the only person behind her was the Rear Senior.

Knowing she was last took the wind out of Michaela's sails. She just couldn't run any more. She stopped and bent over, gasping and out of breath. She fell to her knees. The Rear Senior blew a whistle. Two Senior Race Assistants joined them.

"Stay with her," Michaela heard the Rear Senior say. "I'll go join the runners."

"Are you okay?" a tall senior asked.

Michaela stood up and nodded, still catching her breath.

"Let's get you back to camp, then," said the tall senior. She handed Michaela a bottle of water.

"Every summer there's some newbie who doesn't complete this course," she said to her partner, who snickered.

By the time they arrived at the camp, the race was over. Michaela noticed Team Blue celebrating their win. She could not see her Pink teammates anywhere. She wanted to tell them she was sorry.

Rachel, Bethany and Cindy were waiting for her outside her cabin. They did not look happy.

"Let's take a walk," Rachel said through her teeth. It was more like a command.

Michaela looked at each of them. Her skin prickled with nerves. Yet she was not afraid. She was prepared to fight all three of them, if it came to that.

Bring it on, she thought.

They walked without speaking a word. They stopped

on the beach at the edge of camp and the three girls surrounded Michaela.

"You know what DNF means, don't you?" Rachel asked sarcastically.

Michaela knew what she meant. In running, DNQ was Did Not Qualify. And DNF was Did Not Finish. She nodded.

"Which means you desecrated our sport," Bethany chimed in. "And you embarrassed us, city girl." She twisted her ponytail.

"I'm s —" Michaela started.

"Zip it," Cindy hissed. "Don't wanna hear it."

Bethany laughed out loud like she just heard a joke. Michaela was surprised, until she saw two seniors stroll past them.

"This is what we really, really want, Michaela from the great big city." Rachel took charge again as soon as the seniors had gone. "Here's a little advice. Never run cross-country ever again," She said, pointing at Michaela's face.

"That way, you won't let anybody down," whispered Cindy.

"Totally, stick to track. By yourself, *bronze medalist*," Rachel spat.

"Or kayak through your concrete jungle," Cindy offered.

"Nothing with the word *team*," Bethany said.

"We gave you a chance. But you blew it," Rachel declared.

She signalled to Bethany and Cindy and they all walked away. Michaela stood alone facing the water, peering out to the horizon.

Maybe they're right, she thought. *I'm no cross-country runner.*

2 Not Quite HERSELF

Michaela stepped off the private minibus onto the parking lot. She was at the Cineplex Cinemas at Scarborough Town Centre, on the east side of big-city Toronto. Her parents hurried up to her and hugged her tightly.

"It's so good to have you back, sweetheart," Mom cried. "Welcome home."

"I was only gone for two weeks, not a year."

"Felt like a year," Dad said. "We missed you, that's all."

Michaela did not tell them that she had missed them, too. But she did appreciate Mom taking a vacation day to come pick her up. Mom was always busy with her job as executive director of a women's centre.

It was just past noon on the first Friday in August. It was the beginning of a long weekend.

"I know we were planning to go to the restaurant. But let's pick up the rotis. We can have them on the balcony instead," Michaela suggested.

The whole family loved rotis, large roasted wraps with ground split peas between layers of dough and filled with curry. Mom always ordered shrimp. Although Dad was African American, his favourite was a Caribbean classic — goat.

He drove into their Mornelle Court complex of high-rise apartments with neighbouring townhouses. Michaela thought about how different it was from the sprawling houses on acres of land the girls at camp had described as their homes.

In a short time, the Robinsons were in lounge chairs, wearing sunglasses and sipping mango-passionfruit juice from a pitcher. They sat facing the sun to the south and enjoyed a gentle breeze off Lake Ontario a few kilometres away. Michaela thought they looked like tourists on a hotel balcony. She was happy to be home in their two-bedroom apartment. It felt safe.

"I'm so glad you had a summer camp experience, at last." Mom smiled.

Michaela talked between bites of her roti with bone-less chicken, spinach and chickpeas. She answered her parents' questions about her summer camp activities.

"Kayaking, paddleboarding and archery I under-stand. Zip-lining?" Dad gulped. "You'll never catch me doing that."

"I'd like to try zip-lining someday," Mom said, wiping her mouth.

"Without me," Dad said flatly. "I like seeing the tops of trees from a plane."

Michaela did not mention the words *cross-country running*.

That night, she turned in early. She was glad to be back in her own room. The walls were plastered with posters of female runners from Ghana, Nigeria, USA and Canada. Also, the singers Destra, Beyoncé and Janelle Monáe. The top of her dresser was almost empty. There was a bottle of Reb'l Fleur perfume by Rihanna. Michaela enjoyed a spray of it on weekends and special occasions for its fruity scent. But she was not keen on makeup and didn't have many hair products. From her track days, she kept her black curly hair short. It dried in seconds, and it was one less thing to worry over. Long ago, she saw how other Black girls fussed over their hair for hours and spent whole days in hair salons. She had decided that was not for her.

The next day was going to be a long one. It was a celebration Michaela had waited all year for.

★★★

Michaela is bent over. She takes a long breath and looks ahead towards the last three runners grouped together. She waves off the two Senior Race Assistants ready to help her. She takes off behind the group.

I can catch them, *she thinks.*

With a renewed burst of energy, she bounds along the course. She keeps that last group in her sight. Within seconds, Michaela is almost behind them.

If I can get past them, I won't be last. And I'll finish the race.

The group of runners speeds up. Michaela feels like she is running backwards instead of catching up. The more she tries, the farther ahead of her they run.

I must reach them . . . I must reach . . . *she gasps to herself.*

★★★

Michaela opened her eyes and sat up in bed. She looked over at the clock on her nightstand.

4:04 a.m.

She flopped back onto her pillow. She stared at the ceiling until she drifted off again. No more dreams or nightmares invaded her sleep.

At 6:00 a.m., the sound of wind chimes from Michaela's clock radio woke her. Opening her eyes, she reached over and clicked off her alarm. She remembered where she was, and what day it was. But her body felt like she had run ten 2-K races.

She padded into the kitchen in a light yellow robe. She heard the gentle sounds of steel drums and smelled breakfast. Mom was packing a cooler with the lunch Dad had prepared the day before. Seeing her, Dad pressed the HealthMaster buttons and a green smoothie spun into delicious existence. She greeted her parents and dropped into a chair.

"You look beat," said Dad. "A shower will revive you." He poured the smoothie into three travel bottles.

"I can't make it today," Michaela said.

Mom touched her forehead with the back of her hand.

"I'm not sick, Mom. Only tired. I'll stay and rest."

"Oh, honey, you've been looking forward to the parade all year," Mom said.

"We all have. That's why I want . . . I *insist* you both go. I'll be fine here. Please don't worry about me," she pleaded.

West Indian people called the Toronto Carnival/Caribana by its old name of Caribana. The parade was the crowning moment of a month-long, activity-filled cultural gift to the city. And it was an important part of Michaela's family heritage. Mom was from Trinidad and Tobago, home of the steel drums that Michaela played.

"You've had a very active two weeks," Dad offered. "I understand."

"And you, *young people*, need some entertainment," Michaela said. She stood up and put her smoothie in the fridge for later. "So, go. I'm only a call or text away."

"All right," Mom said. "We'll come back if you need us."

After they left, Michaela slept for a few more hours. Then she had a quick shower and changed into shorts and a T-shirt. She sat in front of the TV, a giant painting of Carnival masqueraders behind her. She nibbled on baked chicken and potato salad with cubed beets.

Michaela's mom texted and Michaela assured her that everything was fine. Then she forced herself to finish her lunch. She had skipped breakfast, and knew she needed some energy to shake that not-quite-herself feeling. And maybe doing something to take her mind off things would help.

She left the apartment, but avoided the elevators. She did not feel like talking if she ran into chatty neighbours. So she jogged down the twelve flights of stairs. She left her bike parked in the basement and strolled east along Ellesmere, crossing the intersection at Morningside. Ten minutes later, she passed the edge of Highland Creek Community Park. Morningside Senior Public School was just to the north. Another month and she would be back there for grade eight.

She entered the Highland Creek branch of Toronto Public Library. Someone had left a book on Canadian Olympic athletes on a table. She flipped through it, catching sight of female sprinters, distance runners and soccer players.

In the young adult section, she pulled out *Batting Brenda*, a girl's cricket novel. She read the blurb on the back cover, thinking of how she had played cricket with her cousins in Brooklyn, New York, a few summers before. And she had watched women's world cup matches on TV with Dad. But there was no cricket team at Morningside. She was not about to switch schools for one year to play cricket.

Her secret favourite reading category was science fiction. Michaela placed two novels on the electronic self-checkout plate and swiped her card under the red-lit reader.

Back at home, she sat on the balcony with her chilled smoothie. She escaped into the magical world of *Brown Girl in the Ring* by Nalo Hopkinson. She paused only to exchange another text with Mom to assure her that she was okay.

Just before Mom and Dad returned home, Michaela recalled the dream of Camp Stone Hearth that had awoken her in the night. She did not like the sensation of reaching for something and not succeeding at grasping it.

"Defeat. That's what it felt like," she said aloud to the empty balcony.

3 Getting in SHAPE

A few days later, Dad knocked on Michaela's bedroom door. Mom had left for work. Michaela was sitting up in bed reading *Batting Brenda*.

"Come in."

Dad opened the door and stood in the doorway. "Care to join me for a jog in the ravine?"

Since he had been laid off from his job, Dad was spending his days applying for new positions. So Michaela was suspicious right away. "You haven't asked me to jog since last spring. And you've lost the twelve pounds Mom was begging you to lose. So what's up?"

"I thought you could use some air."

"I can stand on the balcony."

"And stay home. You haven't wanted to go out, and it's not like you."

Michaela felt a lecture coming on. But Dad was right. Since the long weekend, all she was doing was reading and watching TV.

Summer will be over soon, she thought. "Give me ten minutes."

The sun was high in the blue, cloudless sky as they entered Ellesmere Ravine, west of their apartment building. It had rained during the night. There was a cool breeze, but Michaela knew that it would be hot and humid by noon.

They slowly jogged south, under Ellesmere Road into Morningside Park, then east into Highland Creek Park. Purple, pink and yellow wildflowers were in full bloom. Dad had once told her that the entire Scarborough area was deep country only one hundred years ago. And that the creek was a full river, rushing south-east down to Lake Ontario.

There were no traffic sounds. Only birds. *It's almost like being at camp*, Michaela thought. She felt again the peace she found at Camp Stone Hearth when she enjoyed the quiet wilderness. And then she felt the wave of disappointment when she quit the race, exhausted.

Michaela signalled to Dad. They turned around and headed back north. Then it was time for their cool-down walk.

"Since you returned from summer camp, you haven't been the same," Dad said, breaking the silence.

Michaela could feel him looking at her sideways. She avoided his gaze.

"Your mom has noticed a difference also," he continued.

"You've been talking about me?" she asked, annoyed.

"It's what parents do, sweetheart. We talk about you in front of your face *and* behind your back," he chuckled. "And we've always told you that you can talk about anything with us. Anything at all."

She had wanted to talk to her best friend Kaffy Adebayo about the incident at Camp Stone Hearth. But they would not be able to Skype for a few more weeks. Kaffy was still in Nigeria visiting relatives. And even when she returned home, home wasn't Scarborough any more. Michaela had been heartbroken when Kaffy moved to Buffalo, New York, in June. Keeping her sadness and missing Kaffy inside was like carrying a heavy burden. She knew Mom and Dad were sensing that.

So she told Dad about the cross-country event and what the girls had said to her. Tears were flowing down her face. She wiped them with her forearm. Dad wrapped her to his chest in a hug. She was glad he had listened without interrupting and asking any questions.

"I'm pleased you shared that with me, Michaela," he said as he released her. "Children tease each other. I get it. I was once a child, too."

"Were you?" she asked. Her eyes were wide as she teased him. "I thought all parents were born grown-up."

Dad chuckled as they continued walking. After a while, he said, "That kind of situation is not mere teasing. It's hurtful. And you've carried that hurt for more than a week. Do you think they treated you like that because you're Black?"

"I thought about that. I got the feeling they had checked out other girls. They only asked me because they ran out of choices. And I did have running experience. Even though it was not the right kind."

"Okay. We can rule out race as a basis for their bullying. But they kept calling you 'city girl.'"

"I'm not sure they would have been that mean if I was from the suburbs."

"Or if you had the same kind of wealth. I get it now."

"They saw me as a loner who should not be part of a team."

"Well, you are kind of a loner. That's not always a bad thing. But it's also good to connect with people your own age. Don't let the words of those three girls cause you any more pain. And don't let anyone destroy your desires or steal your joy," Dad advised. "Is cross-country running something you still want to do this fall?"

"I haven't been thinking about it lately."

"You have the free will to make that decision, one way or the other. The past does not determine the future."

"Okay, Dad."

★★★

Two mornings later, Michaela sat with Dad in the living room.

"I've made a decision, Dad," Michaela said. "I've decided not to decide about cross-country yet."

"So . . ."

"I've decided, since school won't start for three weeks, to enjoy running . . . jogging. I want to do it for fun and not feel like I'm competing."

"Sounds like a good plan. It's completely up to you to go after what you want. The key thing to remember, if you do decide to run cross-country at school, is the participation. Not everything is about winning."

"Can we jog tomorrow, Dad?"

"Sorry, I have a job interview. But I don't want you to jog in the ravine by yourself. Whenever I can't go with you, run in the staircase."

And that's what Michaela did. She ran up the twelve flights in the building's staircase. Then she took the elevator down, waited for two minutes and ran back up. She repeated the cycle until she felt she had had enough.

After that day, all through August, Michaela and Dad jogged in the ravine. They went farther and farther each time. On the Friday before the Labour Day long weekend, Michaela insisted that they follow Highland Creek all the way down to Colonel Danforth Park near Lawrence Avenue East.

As they finished their cool-down in Ellesmere Ravine, Dad turned to Michaela. "How do you feel?" he asked.

"Target accomplished."

"I wasn't sure I could keep up with you today. I woke up tired this morning. How do you feel, overall?"

"Better than when we started three weeks ago."

"Your pacing seems much stronger. Sorry that I'm no running coach."

"You've been great, Dad. Encouraging me to get out there. Isn't that coaching? It's been fun. Fun is what I needed," she beamed.

★★★

The next day, Mom and Dad took Michaela to the Canadian National Exhibition. The CNE was another annual summer treat for Michaela. She enjoyed the rides and sampled treats from all over the world in the food building.

That evening she finally got to Skype with Kaffy. They caught up on their summers.

"I missed you so much today, Kaffy," said Michaela.

"Only today? Girl, I missed you the whole summer. I wish I'd been on those crazy rides at the Ex."

"How was your trip to Nigeria?"

"Really nice. Good to see my grandparents and all those relatives. And to eat fruits right from the tree again."

Michaela told Kaffy about summer camp and the racing incident. Then she announced, "I'm thinking of trying out for the cross-country team."

"Thinking of? That doesn't sound like a real decision."

"What if I'm not good at it?"

"So what? If you suck at it, call a press conference and give back the six million they're paying you. But keep the gold running shoes."

Michaela chuckled.

"You won't know until you do it."

"You're right, Kaffy."

"Don't let anyone or anything hold you back. Who knows, you might even have fun and make friends. Though they won't be as amazing as your old friend."

"Same for you at your new school. Show them that a true African American can have a Canadian accent."

They said goodbye and Michaela closed her laptop. She thought about how they learned goal-setting in school. That it was an important part of starting something new. She grabbed a piece of paper and wrote four goals on it. Then she pinned it to her cork board and read her goals aloud:

"One: Make the cross-country team.

Two: Become a top-ten runner by the end of the season.

Three: Finish every race I start, even if I collapse at the end.

Four: Never let down my team."

But first, she had to get *on* the team.

4 TRYOUTS

Tuesday. First day back at school. Michaela was dressed in a new uniform. A moss-green golf shirt with Morningside Senior Public School's monogram over her heart, gray slacks and brand new running shoes. She would alternate the shoes with her older ones. She rode her bike across the north-side sidewalk of Ellesmere to school.

Before the first school buzzer rang, Michaela went to the front office to get the name of the new Grade Eight cross-country coach. At the top of her lunch period, she left her sandwich and smoothie in her locker. She knocked on the coach's office door on the lower level.

"Come in."

Michaela entered and closed the door behind her.

The woman stood up behind her desk and held out her tanned hand. "I'm Ms. Bedard," she said. Her hair was short and almost spiky, and a colour Michaela guessed would be called auburn.

"Michaela Robinson," she responded as she shook

the hand. She noticed a half-eaten bowl of salad and a bottle of apple juice on the desk. "May I have a really short meeting with you, Ms. Bedard?"

"I can give you ten minutes." The coach waved her into the chair directly in front of Michaela.

"Ms. Bedard, I'd like to try out for the girls' cross-country team."

"Wow! I haven't even posted a schedule yet. And you're the second girl to come in here. Do you know Belinda Troutman?"

Michaela shook her head.

"She was waiting outside the door before I arrived this morning. Have you run cross-country before, Michaela?"

Michaela told her about her sprint seasons in track. She did not think one half-race at summer camp counted for cross-country experience. She did not mention jogging with Dad in case it sounded lame. It wasn't racing experience.

"Cross-country is quite different from sprinting, Michaela. But you bring speed from track, so starting and finishing strong are assets in your toolbox."

Toolbox? Michaela wondered. *She must mean set of skills.*

"You coming in here shows a determined personality. That's a good thing to have. Tryouts begin this Thursday. Mornings only at eight a.m. sharp. No lateness. Rain or shine. Weekends, you're on your own. Selection day is in two weeks, if you make it 'til then. It's not for the faint-hearted." She held Michaela's gaze and continued. "Team of five. Four key positions plus an alternate. Alternate's points don't count in races. Unless they happen to place above one of the key runners. And that's rare. Questions?"

Michaela looked around the small office. There were posters of pro distance runners she didn't recognize. She looked back at Ms. Bedard, who was wearing a white frilly blouse with tan dress slacks.

No track suit? Michaela wondered. "Do you teach phys. ed.?" she asked.

"French and drama. If you're wondering what makes me qualified to coach cross-country, I'll say years of 10-K races, which I still do. And I've coached Grade Seven and Eight cross-country runners at another school."

"I didn't mean to offend you . . ."

"No offence taken. A fair question. I encourage questions. Anything else?" As she waited for a response, she handed Michaela a set of stapled forms with Permission on the top.

As Michaela reached out for them, she noticed a quote stencilled on a wall of the office: "*You Form Your Own Destiny From Within Yourself.*"

"Nothing else, Ms. Bedard," Michaela stood, smiling. "Thank you."

"I hope to see you on Thursday," Coach Bedard

said, returning the smile. As she plunged a fork into her salad, Michaela opened the door and exited.

You will, she thought.

Morningside's character trait for September was *Fairness*. All Michaela hoped for was a fair chance at making the team.

★★★

It was 7:45 a.m. on Thursday. Michaela had the permission forms signed by Dad and ready to hand in to Coach Bedard as she walked onto the small track.

The boys' and girls' soccer teams were already at either half of the field in practice. Michaela headed to the northern edge of Highland Creek Community Park. Only one girl was there. She was stretching. They nodded to each other.

"Hi. I'm Belinda," said the stranger.

"Michaela."

Other girls and boys ran towards them. They all began their stretches. Some chatted to each other. Michaela stretched her legs.

A whistle blew in three short bursts.

Michaela turned to see Coach Bedard in sweatpants, a T-shirt and running shoes, and carrying a clipboard. A few more boys and girls arrived, puffing hard, and everyone handed her their permission forms.

Coach Bedard looked at her watch and blew her

whistle once more. She gestured for everyone to gather closer. "Good morning, cross-country runners. I'm Coach Bedard."

"And I'm Coach Mazzocato," a male voice boomed. Michaela turned to see a man Dad would call "rake thin," with sandy blond hair and bright blue eyes.

The students were divided into groups. Coach Mazzocato took the Grade Seven girls and boys off to one side of the park. Coach Bedard remained with the Grade Eight girls and boys. As she took attendance, Michaela counted fourteen girls.

I'll have to beat at least ten of them to make the team, she thought. *I wonder if I can.*

Coach Bedard led them in a quick group stretch. "This is one area of your running that you never skip and that you never cheat yourself on," she said. "Consider it a gift to your body. For those of you new to running or new to cross-country running, keep these things in mind: One, warm-up stretch. Two, warm-up jog. Three, the run. Four, cool-down jog. Five, cool-down stretch." She counted the steps off on her fingers.

The Grade Sevens had started their warm-up jog by the time Coach Bedard took the Grade Eights to the western edge of the park.

"Four loops of the park equals three kilometres, which is your race distance," she instructed. "All you girls and boys will jog the warm-up together. Then you will run separately. Afterwards, you cool down and stretch together. From here, you'll go down the western trail between the trees to Ellesmere Road. Turn left, keeping on the grass to the eastern edge. Turn left again and come back up on the path. Turn left once more and across to this area. Got it?"

They nodded.

"There are orange cones along the course, especially on the corners. Always keep to the right of them. Any questions?"

A girl raised her hand. "Who starts first when we race, girls or boys?"

"Girls. But you're training together in a group for now," Coach Bedard replied.

Michaela recognized the girl from phys. ed. the day before. Her name was Hennie. The teacher had mentioned she was from Saskatoon, Saskatchewan. He had called her a *stubble jumper*, explaining that it meant one who moved away from the province. Michaela had not been sure about joining the others in laughter until she saw Hennie giggling.

The Grade Eight girls and boys finished their two-loop warm-up. Then Coach Bedard had them rest for two minutes. She blew her whistle and the girls began their 3-K run. Michaela kept up with them, although she remained near the back of the pack.

Day one of ten tryout days was over.

Michaela was on the hunt for a place on the team. And it felt good.

5 Jockeying for POSITION

By Tuesday morning, there were thirteen Grade Eight girls left trying out because one girl had twisted her ankle. By Friday, Michaela heard it whispered that the girl who constantly came in last had quit. That left twelve girls who wanted a place on the team. Michaela was now running near the middle of the pack. Even though Coach Bedard said that their runs were not really races, she knew differently. A feeling of competition filled the air.

Michaela had not yet finished in the top five. It was beginning to worry her.

That Saturday, Michaela and Dad started running in Ellesmere Ravine. She set the pace based on how she had been running during the week. They made it all the way down past Colonel Danforth Park and Lawrence Avenue East to Lake Ontario.

They rested before running back up and cooling down in the Ellesmere Ravine area.

"Are you trying to commit patricide, child?" Dad panted.

"What's that?"

"A child killing her poor dad . . . before his time."

Dad leaned against a tree, chuckling. He had not jogged in the past two weeks. Michaela's pace had increased. This was serious running.

"I think we ran a 3-K twice," Michaela said, catching her breath. "Let's do it again."

Dad shot her a killer glare.

"I'm kidding," she said.

★★★

The evening before selection day, Michaela picked at her supper. Mom was working late.

She's always working late these days, Michaela thought.

"Food will give you nourishment," Dad said between mouthfuls of vegetable lasagna.

"I know." She put down her fork. "We're down to nine girls trying out. Today, I finished seventh. I was behind this girl who always wears a red headband. The top three girls seem to be in a world of their own. Always way ahead."

"You're no stranger to racing, Michaela. Think back to your 400-metre days."

"This is different!" she exploded.

"Hear me out. When you ran the 400, everyone would be almost together for the first 200, maybe 250 metres. Then you would decide to make your move.

Jump into a higher gear before the final turn on the track. If you were leading, you still found that extra gear to extend your lead. If you were behind three or four girls, you knew who to aim for. And there was always someone behind who could overtake you."

"Strategy."

"Exactly. You don't have to *win* tomorrow. You need to *place*. Look, you've already proven your summer camp critics wrong. You've picked yourself up and trained relentlessly. By gaining a spot, you'll be able to help others on your team."

"Only if I'm one of the top four. The alternate's points don't count in races. I'm nervous," she admitted.

"Nervous is good. It means you're alive. I get nervous and my palms sweat before an important meeting or a presentation. Use the nerves to do your best."

"All right, Dad." She picked up her fork again.

"Finish your food," he said. "I'll race you." He shovelled two forkfuls of food into his mouth.

That night, Michaela fell asleep with Dad's words echoing in her head. The next morning, she stood under the shower. For the last minute, she switched from hot to cool water. That was a trick Dad had taught her a long time ago.

"You might start your shower sleepy," he had said. "But you'll end it fully awake, trust me."

By the time Michaela had dressed and entered the

kitchen, Mom had already left for work. Dad had another interview. There was a note on the table:

Have a great run.

Love, Mom and Dad.

She tucked it into her pants pocket. She had followed her morning routine of drinking a glass of water as soon as she was up. Now she drank some orange juice and ate a banana and a McIntosh apple. She would eat one of two sandwiches Mom prepared, along with a snack of celery sticks, after the race. As usual, she put an extra pair of socks, along with a fresh towel, in her backpack.

Soon, nine nervous, excited and determined girls stood along an invisible line at the north end of Highland Creek Community Park. Coach Bedard blew her whistle and off they went. Belinda quickly took the lead. The grass was still damp with dew, and slippery in places.

Michaela ran in the middle of the pack. She was always aware of her position in relation to the other runners. Melanie challenged and took the lead as they completed the second loop and headed south once more.

Things remained that way until the top of the last loop. Michaela counted six girls ahead of her. The pace was quickening. Hennie was beside Belinda as they turned east. Michaela was trying to decide when to make a move.

At the turn north, Belinda took the lead and passed Melanie along the paved path. Then she began to extend her lead. Michaela moved up alongside Alice, the girl with the red headband. They both passed two girls at the same time. There were now gaps separating Belinda, Melanie and Hennie. Michaela knew that after the final turn there would be a 60-metre sprint to the finish line.

The gaps became even wider. Alice kept up the pace on her left.

She realized she couldn't catch Hennie. *Remember your strategy*, she told herself.

Fifth would be the alternate position. She wanted a firm spot on the team. She wanted her points to count in races.

Michaela and Alice made the final turn still together. Driven, Michaela kicked into high gear and sprinted towards the finish line. She didn't look back. But as she collapsed onto the wet grass, she knew that she had edged out Alice for a spot on the team.

★★★

The next morning, Friday, was the first formal team meeting. They gathered in an empty classroom at 8:00 a.m. After introductions, Coach Bedard said, "Girls and boys, I repeat, you will be training alongside each other. But don't think that you are competing against each other, okay? I will not tolerate that nonsense."

This time Michaela took a real look at the girls who were now her teammates. For the past two weeks they had been merely bodies next to her. No friendships had been formed. Michaela noticed that Belinda and Melanie did not say much to each other. Both had been on the Grade Seven cross-country team the year before.

Sitting in the large circle, Michaela observed her teammates. Belinda Troutman was captain and number 1, and the fastest. She had long black hair with a purple streak and wore earrings with a tiny feather dangling from each. She was long-limbed and tall like Michaela. Michaela had overheard the Grade Eight boys' captain, Jason Puerta, say that Belinda could become a top-three podium runner.

Number 2 was Melanie Mackenzie with her long reddish hair. She did not look happy when Coach Bedard named Belinda as captain.

Number 3 was Hennie Janssen. Michaela had noticed that she seemed focused in gym class and very serious about running. Number 5, the alternate, was Alice Takahashi, the girl with the red hairband. She was now Michaela's closest rival. She had sparkling eyes that had given Michaela a long stare after their race.

These four girls have been running cross-country for longer than I have, Michaela thought. *I'm the newbie. I have to keep proving myself to stay on this team.*

"Okay, we have a short season," Coach Bedard began. "All races will be on Thursday afternoons."

"Any weekend practices, Coach?" asked Melanie.

"Weekends, you're still on your own. Mondays will be your rest day, unless I need to change it," Coach Bedard responded. "Questions?"

"Why do you enter 10-K races?" Michaela wanted to know.

"To keep up my fitness," Coach Bedard replied. "Although some of them are non-competitive. I get to raise funds for charities and causes like the Terry Fox Run this Sunday."

Michaela was suddenly reminded of Dad saying that everything was not about winning. *Maybe he meant something like that*, she thought.

Coach Bedard handed out sheets of paper. "Here is the course map for Thompson Memorial Park. You will have a practice run next week. Then a qualifier before the North Conference Final. I expect you to do well at each. And if we're lucky this year, City Finals."

She looked at each of them, letting the information sink in.

"Morningside has not had a Grade Eight girls' or boys' team at City Finals for three years," she continued. "I hope to change that this year."

"How many teams in the City Finals, Coach?" Hennie asked.

"Sixteen. The top-four finalists from each quadrant in the city. Northwest, Southwest, Southeast and Northeast."

Coach Bedard showed them a three-minute video of middle school girls starting two different races. Next, she showed one of middle school boys starting two races. There was much chatter among the group. Then she settled them down.

"Today's exercise is about starting a race. Close your eyes," Coach Bedard began. "Picture yourself at the starting line. There might be sixty or eighty of you. Not everyone will be at the front. Don't let that bother you. You want to start the first 200 metres clean. No elbowing. No tripping or falling, either. Focus on a clean, safe start. Then settle into running your own race for yourself and your team."

Michaela, eyes closed, tried to focus. The summer camp race kept flashing across her brain.

Will I ever get past it? she wondered.

6 Practice RACE

It was a dry afternoon in late September. The calendar said it was fall, yet the air was still warm. Michaela thought of the mental exercise on having a clean start to her race. She stared out the bus window.

The orange school bus cruised past her Mornelle Court complex and climbed the long hill towards Neilson Road. It stopped at the traffic lights by the plaza where her family shopped at the Food Basics, Dollarama and Tim Hortons. On the opposite side was Centenary Hospital where Michaela was born.

All of this was a blur today.

The chatter-filled school bus carried the four Morningside teams. It dipped down a hill, up again across Military Trail, then picked up speed past Markham Road, Bellamy and McCowan.

Alice was sitting in the seat beside Michaela. They had not said a word to each other. Michaela kept thinking about what she could do with her team, the way Coach Bedard helped charities. Then her mind shifted again to the starting line and her running strategy — not too fast at the start. But not too slow, either.

The bus turned south onto Brimley. They were minutes away from Thompson Memorial Park. The chatter increased. Michaela remembered the park from picnics with her parents at Sunday afternoon steelpan *limes* — get togethers — before Caribana.

Her mind came back to the present as other school buses came into view in the parking lot.

"Good luck, today," Alice said to Michaela.

"You, too," Michaela replied.

They headed to the area Michaela always called *Tent City*, a group of open tents for schools and officials to store their gear.

Fifteen Northeast Conference Grade Eight teams were bunched together at the starting line, to the east of the baseball diamond. They stood about ten across. Michaela stood in the middle, wearing her Morningside singlet over a white T-shirt. Her registration number was written on the back of her hand with a marker. She bounced on the balls of her feet.

Because there were houses close to the park, a course marshall used a large red flag instead of a starter's pistol. He lifted it to get the runners ready. Seconds later, he brought it down.

The runners were off in a stampede. Michaela smiled as she thought of a news clip of the running of the bulls in Spain. Men, dressed in white with red handkerchiefs around their necks and red scarves around their waists, were chased through the streets by bulls. Some fell and were helped up. Some were gored by the horns of the bulls. Spectators cheered.

Who's chasing us? she thought. *Not bulls. No one. But we're all running as if our lives depended on it.*

The course soon narrowed up a paved incline, heading north. It had been a clean, safe start for Michaela. She was pleased with that.

Stay with the pack. Finish the race. One loop down. One more to go.

Then she no longer saw the leaders. Hennie was not that far ahead of her. Looking back, she saw Alice's red headband.

They crossed a bridge and entered a trail flanked by trees again. The leaves had begun to change colour with splotches of yellow and orange.

If I can catch Hennie, I'll be in a good position.

Suddenly, she could not see Alice behind her.

Did she pass me? Or did she fall further behind? Keep going, Michaela.

They were quickly turning from the dog park at the south end into the final all-grass stretch. Everyone seemed to be sprinting, Michaela included. She was disoriented after she crossed the finish line and entered the funnel. Marked with wood posts and rope, this area kept the runners in their order to record their placements. As someone checked the number on the back of Michaela's hand, she knew that lots of runners had come in before her and her teammates.

She was still in a daze when they gathered to cheer on the Grade Eight boys for the last race.

★★★

The Grade Eight girls' team placed seventh. They were somber at the next Friday morning meeting. Only the top six teams would qualify for the Northeast Conference Finals.

"Okay, it was a practice run," Coach Bedard said. "Don't look so glum, girls. I know that you'll do better next week because each of you posted better times in practice. Leave the past behind you."

Michaela felt she should have done better. She had done better than Alice. But not well enough to help the team.

"The course was tougher than when we ran in grade seven," Melanie offered.

"Yes, that's how courses are," Coach Bedard explained. "One day they'll have you wading chest-high across a river."

"Really?" Alice asked innocently.

Melanie and Hennie both turned and stared at Alice.

"I'm kidding," Coach Bedard replied. "Seriously,

one good thing about yesterday is that you got a sense of your competition."

"I think we got a strong sense of how we need to pace ourselves," Belinda said.

"Very perceptive, captain," Coach Bedard beamed. "This weekend I want you all to do longer distances. And be mindful of your breathing."

"What about after school today?" Melanie asked.

"What about it? Got a hot date?" Coach Bedard asked.

Melanie blushed and shook her head. Two of the boys giggled.

"This afternoon, speed work. Okay, why do you run?"

"To get to the other side," Jason quipped.

Everyone laughed.

"Why do we run, runners?" she repeated.

"To challenge ourselves," Belinda said.

"Yeah. We exercise to feel good," Hennie replied.

"To get better and better," Alice added.

"Good. Who else runs?" Coach Bedard then asked.

"Politicians," Melanie said.

"Yeah, like . . . school trustees, too," Hennie added.

"Yes, they run for office," Coach Bernard admitted. "But that's not the kind of running we're talking about."

"Soccer players," Michaela offered. She wondered why the boys hardly said anything when they were all together.

"Football players," Hennie said.

"Baseball players. Around the bases," Alice said.

"Field hockey players," Melanie said.

"Lacrosse players," Belinda shared.

"Good, people." Coach Bedard smiled. "Do golfers run?"

"No. But they could if they wanted to," Colin, alternate for the boys' team, spoke up. "Swing the golf club, run down the fairway. Hey, maybe that's the new way to play the game."

A few chuckled.

"There has to be a purpose behind it," Coach Bedard explained. "Some run to achieve something. For themselves. For a country. What's your purpose? You don't have to answer out loud. Let it sit with you. You've been running for yourselves. Girls. Boys. Combine that drive inside you for your team also. Remember that you're a team. Questions?"

Coach Bedard's words reminded Michaela of what Dad had said: not everything is about winning. And Michaela had been thinking all week about Coach Bedard running in the Terry Fox Run. Now she knew a way to share her drive with the team. She raised her hand. Coach Bedard pointed at her.

"The Helping Hand Food Drive has started. Different groups are collecting food items for their headquarters," she said. "I suggest that the cross-country teams hold a bake sale. And we donate the money raised."

"How much time will that take?" Melanie asked. "We're all very busy."

"Will we have to bake stuff ourselves?" Jason asked.

"Whenever I bake anything, it burns," Hennie stated.

"Do you have a plan, Michaela?" Coach Bedard asked.

Michaela laid out her plan in detail, that everyone would bake something at home, then bring it in to school on sale day. Michaela would promote it on the morning announcements. Everyone listened.

"If you can't bake, join up with someone who can," she concluded. "I'll speak to Coach Mazzocato about the Grade Sevens, if you guys agree."

"Sounds good to me," Coach Bedard said. "Let's take a vote."

Alice's hand shot up. Then a few more. There was huddling between two pairs. Eventually, all hands were raised.

"Very nice. If the Grade Sevens agree, it's a go," Coach Bedard said. "Okay, let's talk about the middle of the course. I think it's where most of you had your challenges. And this applies to you boys as well."

I hope Dad has some free time this weekend, Michaela thought as they started going over the race plan.

★★★

For supper Dad baked his famous jerk salmon steaks, along with a twelve-piece salad. Michaela told him how good everything tasted. Mom seemed to have something on her mind. Michaela figured it might be something to do with her work.

Michaela went to her room to do some of her homework so she could focus on running and relaxing over the weekend. Soon she heard Mom and Dad arguing. Leaving the homework, she unzipped her tenor steel drum from its case and set up its metal frame. One thing Mom and Dad never complained about was her practising at home.

While the vocal storm raged down the hallway, Michaela tuned up the steel drum and decided what to play. Her solo repertoire included the national anthems of Canada, USA, Trinidad and Tobago, and South Africa. Also various calypsos and pop tunes. She chose a classic, Machel Montano's "She Ready."

She found it soothing from all the week's excitement. And it drowned out her parents arguing.

7 Scouting the COURSE

The morning air was still cool when Michaela and Dad finished stretching. Dad held the course map on the car's hood in the parking lot at Thompson Memorial Park.

"We don't have to be exact, Dad," said Michaela as they studied the map. "I remember some of it from Thursday."

"You're the pro, Michaela. If we get lost, you call 911, not me."

Michaela laughed. She tried to be in a good mood, despite some troubling thoughts.

They sauntered over to the starting area.

"On-your-mark-get-set-go!" Michaela shouted.

They jogged side by side. Michaela seemed to follow the course from muscle memory. Her body knew the twists and turns through the trees and the open stretches. They breezed past senior walkers and other joggers.

"Is Mom still joining us for breakfast at Crepes 'N Pancakes after her yoga class?"

"Of course, sweetheart. Why do you ask?"

"Last night, you two were arguing really loud."

"Yeah . . . we were. But that was couple stuff. It doesn't affect us as a family. We can still sit down and eat together."

Michaela was silent for a while. They were halfway through the loop.

"Is Mom pressuring you to get a job?"

Dad had worked as a manager for a company until his division was moved to Mexico. Everyone was laid off, including Dad.

He looked over at Michaela. Then he stared straight ahead. She could tell he was deciding whether to tell her the truth.

"You remember I told you that the company gave me a package . . . a sum of money . . ."

"You took us to Roti, Curry and Pepper buffet."

"Well, we're still good money-wise. Don't worry. Your mom's just worried that the longer I don't work, the harder it will be for me to land a good job."

Michaela had been wondering if Dad would ever work again. After all, it had been three months.

"Next Monday, Tuesday and Wednesday I'll be in a workshop," he went on. "On career exploration. To examine my skills . . . to have even more chances of landing a solid job." He seemed to be trying to reassure her.

"Good idea, Dad. Because I don't want you to get laid off again." Michaela was still worried, and the argument between her parents made her a bit anxious. But she knew Dad hadn't been slacking. He used his extra time to help Mom around the apartment and do errands. He even baked multigrain bread every weekend. He was looking out for the family. She decided not to ask anything else, for now.

"I'll be at your qualifier on Thursday," he said with a smile. "Got to see my girl in action. Cross . . . country . . . runneeeer!"

She smiled back at him. It would be the first time he would see her race in this new sport.

With the warm-up done, Michaela stretched. Then she peeled off her sweats, down to a T-shirt and shorts for race conditions. She planned to run two loops — 3-K, at her own racing pace, with Dad trailing a short distance behind her for security.

"Bang!" Dad shouted.

Michaela decided to use one of Coach Bedard's exercises. She imagined that she was near the front group of runners, keeping up with them throughout the course. At times, she sped up, passing invisible runners.

One loop down, one to go.

Halfway through the second loop, she decided to make her move.

Soon I'm alongside Hennie. She looks at me, surprised. We both catch up with Melanie, who looks downright dumbfounded. The three of us line up with Belinda, who does a double-take. Make that a triple-take. We enter the home stretch. All four of us are sprinting past the other runners. A 1, 2, 3, 4, finish.

Dad caught up to her.

"Strong finish, sweetheart."

If only you knew, she thought.

They took a short break and Michaela took small sips from her water bottle. Then they ran the 3-K course once more. This time she burst across the finish line first, leaving the entire field of imaginary runners behind her.

Michaela and Dad had completed their cool-down and stretching when a blue Tesla pulled into the parking lot. Belinda hopped out. She was followed by two adults Michaela guessed were her parents. Her dad had a long ponytail. And her mom wore earrings just like Belinda's with a feather dangling from the end. All were wearing sweats.

Belinda ran over to Michaela and they exchanged hellos. Introductions were made all around.

While the adults chatted, Belinda pulled Michaela off to one side.

"Did you run already?" Belinda asked.

"Yeah, I beat my dad both times. Old people are sooo slow," she smiled.

"You ran the course twice? No way."

"Yes, way."

"That's cool. Not every runner thinks to check out the course on their own, let alone come and run it twice. Listen, we're coming back here tomorrow. You want to join me?"

"Sure, Belinda."

They made the arrangements. Michaela left the park with a smile across her face.

★★★

They decided that Belinda would set the pace for a long run Coach Bedard had suggested. They were in the middle of loop number six of six. Michaela was feeling the burn in her calves. So far, it had been tough keeping up with Belinda. Nine kilometres straight.

No wonder she's a top-ten runner, Michaela thought.

Michaela wanted to quit. But she kept telling herself that this was how she was becoming a better runner.

"Hang in there, Michaela."

She's reading my thoughts, now?

Michaela looked back and saw that Belinda's parents were still shadowing them.

"Home stretch," Belinda panted.

Michaela vowed that she was never doing this again. *Belinda's not sticking to this month's character trait of Fairness*, she thought. She remembered Dad accusing her of trying to kill him and thought, *This is destruction of an innocent cross-country runner.*

Finally, they crossed the finish line.

"Don't stop, Michaela. Walk it out."

"Let me lie here and sleep till tomorrow. Pleeease."

Michaela put her hand to her heart. She had never felt it beat so hard. Belinda took her arm and they kept moving. They jogged and walked until they had cooled down.

Belinda's parents joined them with bottles of water and their sweats.

"Good run, girls," Mrs. Troutman beamed.

"If I was your daughter, I'd be dead in a week," Michaela said as she pulled on her sweatpants.

"It's in the blood," Mr. Troutman said. "Cherokee."

"And Mohawk," Mrs. Troutman said.

"That makes me a Mo-Kee," Belinda said. She smiled at the puzzled look on Michaela's face and shoved her playfully before sipping some water.

"I get it," Michaela smiled.

"Our ancestors used to run from Canada down to Miami every year before the winter," Mr. Troutman said with a straight face.

"Children. Elders. Even the dogs," Mrs. Troutman offered.

"And then they took the plane back up in the spring, eh," Belinda added. "The original snow birds."

Michaela looked at them and saw slow grins appearing on their faces.

"Actually, we never pushed Belinda to run. She pushes herself," Mrs. Troutman said.

Now she pushes me, Michaela thought, uncapping her bottle of water.

8 Just Have FUN

Morningside's character trait for October was *Kindness*.

But that week, it seemed to Michaela that Coach Bedard had attended the Brutal School of Belinda. The coach pushed the teams harder than the week before. If they did not qualify, it was going to be a very short season indeed.

Michaela realized that cross-country running was like a tonic. She wanted to taste more. She banged out most of her homework and assignments during lunch or early in the morning before leaving for practice. Each evening she crashed into bed fast asleep with fatigue. No TV. No steel drum playing. No texting. She felt like she was training for the Olympics.

Fall arrived almost overnight. It was like Thompson Memorial Park had been sprayed by a giant with garden hoses of multi-coloured paint from above. At least, that was how the trees appeared to Michaela when she stepped off the school bus for the qualifier.

"Okay, I want you girls to have fun. Running is a fun activity," Coach Bedard began. She was in a huddle with the girls' team. "And I want you to remember what's at stake here. A good team placement and you move on. I have a good feeling. Pass the runner in front of you, and the next, and the next."

"Okay, Coach," they responded in unison.

Two schools that had skipped the practice run now lined up with the rest of the teams. Michaela crouched in the middle of eighty-four jittery girls.

The course marshall lifted a large red flag to get the runners ready. Seconds later, he brought it down.

Michaela followed Belinda's advice. Whenever she reached a clearing, she picked off runners. Others passed her like they were using the same tactic. But Michaela felt she had more control than before. More strength too. She glimpsed cheering Morningside Grade Sevens along the course.

Near the end of the second loop, she looked back to see Alice's red headband bobbing. She surged forward. With 300 metres to go, she saw Dad.

"Sprint it out, Michaela, sprint it out," he shouted over the voices of the other parents.

That was her plan. Yet she took Dad's urging like a power shot of vitamins. A strange thought entered her head as she burst across the finish line.

I'm ready to do this again.

★★★

Coach Bedard gathered them together to celebrate. Then they joined the Morningside Grade Sevens to cheer on the Grade Eight boys' team.

The results were announced. All four Morningside teams had qualified for the Northeast Conference Finals. The Grade Eight girls had placed fourth of the top six teams.

The Friday morning team meeting continued the giddy feelings. They had crossed the first major hurdle. Once more, they sat in a circle.

"I am so pleased that each of you girls broke your personal best times. Alice, I know that, as alternate, your position did not count. But you made a major improvement. Keep it up. You are an asset to this team," Coach Bedard stated.

The others applauded. Alice smiled. Michaela was genuinely happy for her. She realized that Alice was pushing her to be better. *If Alice was not on the team, would I be working as hard?* Michaela wondered.

"I have some news," Coach Bedard continued. "The Beaches Invitational Cross-Country Meet is hosted in the Southeast Conference every year for Grade Seven and Eight girls. This year one Northeast Conference qualifier was picked out of a hat."

"And it's Morningside," Belinda screamed. Her announcement was followed by loud cheers.

"When is it?" Melanie asked.

"Captain. Fill them in," Coach Bedard gestured to Belinda.

"Next Thursday. A blind course."

"What's that?" Michaela asked.

Melanie, Hennie and Alice turned and looked at her.

Yep. I'm still the new girl, she thought.

"I ran one of those last year in Saskatoon. It's a meet where no one knows the course ahead of time," Hennie explained. "Except that it covers different surfaces. We had gravel tracks, dirt tracks and long stretches of high grass. We crossed two creeks and climbed a muddy hill."

"That's right," Belinda agreed. "Since it's in the Beaches, we can guess it will include running on sand, which will be difficult. Unless it rains the night before. There's the boardwalk. And asphalt."

"The asphalt would be the bicycle trail. I've ridden there. It's way cool," Melanie said.

Michaela recalled running on firm sand at summer camp, and felt a twinge of worry.

"We'll be running against the six teams that have already qualified for their Southeast Conference Finals," Belinda concluded.

She looked over to Coach Bedard, who said, "That means you will see only some of those girls again at City Finals."

"If we're lucky," Melanie said.

"*When* we're lucky," Hennie corrected, ruffling her hair.

"Boys, don't feel left out. Coach Mazzocato will take you and the Grade Sevens to Thompson Memorial Park for a special practice next Thursday," Coach Bedard reassured them.

"We'll miss you, girls," Jason said, pretending to cry into his sleeve.

"Okay, you've been working hard lately," Coach Bedard said. "The body needs proper rest. I want you all to take it easy this weekend. Some long runs at very slow pace. We start practice again on Monday. Okay, pair up for a visualization exercise."

Melanie chose Michaela.

"Sit beside your partner and take their hand. Close your eyes."

They all did so.

"Cross-country running can sometimes feel like a lonely sport. Imagine that you're on a long empty road. Like a country road. Trees on either side. The air is fresh."

Michaela flashed to the road at camp. She quickly replaced it with another setting.

"You have a buddy running alongside you, supporting you. Telling you that you're doing just fine. That you have endless energy. That you will make it to the end of the road. Your body responds. You breathe easily. No aches in your legs. Your feet lightly touch the road. Your buddy keeps holding your hand, never letting it go. You keep running. It's the best feeling. Remember that feeling as you open your eyes. Wide awake. Take a slow, deep breath. Turn and thank your partner."

Coach is so creative, Michaela thought. She was starting to really like Coach Bedard's visualization exercises.

9 Helping HANDS

Monday afternoon's speed work was different. One loop of Highland Creek Community Park was just under 800 metres. Coach Bedard gathered the ten girls and boys at the starting point.

"Okay, this is a relay exercise. Belinda and Jason, you will start together." Coach Bedard handed each a metal baton. "You sprint 400 metres to the marker down there. Then you pass the batons to Michaela and Hennie, who will be waiting. You two sprint and pass to Melanie and Alice, right here, who pass on to the boys. Got it?"

They all grunted that they understood.

"The first time you do it, imagine that you're at the start of a race," she instructed. "The next time imagine you are ending the race. The good news is you get to rest in-between at your spots until the baton comes back to you."

When everyone was in position, Coach Bedard blew her whistle.

Afterwards, Michaela was glad that Hennie was her partner for the exercise. It gave them more chance to talk than during their shared gym class. Michaela felt she was starting to get to know her teammate.

At home, after a shower and supper, Dad laid out all the ingredients he had bought from Food Basics for the upcoming bake sale. She inspected every item like a head baker.

"Everything to your liking, Chef?" Dad asked.

"Yes, Master Shopper. You done good. Correction, you did very well. You'll receive a bonus on Father's Day."

"But, Chef, why do I have to wait so long for a well-earned bonus? Thanksgiving, Christmas, Kawnzaa, Valentine's, Family Day, Easter and my birthday all come before Father's Day next year."

"Your argument is sound, Master Shopper. Christmas, it will be."

Dad raised his finger as if to protest but then clearly changed his mind. He sat at the kitchen table and opened a book.

"What are you reading now?" Michaela asked.

"It's about leadership."

"You're already a leader, Dad."

"There's always more to learn on planet Earth."

"Even when I'm sixty-five?"

"Even when you're one hundred and five. Get baking."

Michaela measured, poured, coloured, mixed, tasted, spooned onto cookie sheets and slid trays into the pre-heated oven.

Michaela wondered why Dad wasn't helping her with the baking. He hadn't had any problem doing the shopping. *He's here in case anything goes wrong*, she thought. *I guess he wants me to do it on my own. Like running.*

Dad waved clouds of flour from the air in front of him. Soon, the oven timer dinged. Michaela, wearing oven mitts, eased the first batch out of the oven. Closing the book with a marker in place, Dad sniffed the air.

"Smells right," he said. "As the Official Taste Tester, I am ready for the first bite, Chef."

"These are very expensive," she said. She broke a large cookie into two pieces. "You may taste one half."

Dad munched thoughtfully. He smacked his lips and made humming sounds. The only thing he did not do was gargle bits of cookie.

"*Ladha Bora! Excellent*, in Swahili," he proclaimed. "Good visual appeal. The grated coconut has beautiful colour. There's the right hint of vanilla essence. A wonderful . . . ummm balance of coconut and oatmeal. For the next batch, a little more nutmeg, please, Chef."

"The price just went up by a nickel."

★★★

The next morning, Michaela walked to school extra early. She carried a cardboard box filled with her Pink Coconut Oatmeal Cookies. She checked that all the other baked goods had arrived. They were stored like treasure in Coach Bedard's office before practice.

As part of her detailed plan, Michaela had written the bake sale announcement. She had read it out every morning over the past week over the school's speakers. She wanted an extra nudge today.

***

Principal Venkatramanan said, "Special announcement. During lunch periods today, the Grade Seven and Eight cross-country teams will be holding a bake sale in the cafeteria. If possible, have change available. This is to benefit the Helping Hand Food Drive." She added, "I urge to you support them. Please stand for the playing of 'O, Canada.'"

Michaela's English teacher allowed her to leave class early to set up. Coach Bedard and Belinda came to help. Together, they laid out trays filled with the baked goods, along with place cards. These listed the ingredients, in case of food sensitivities. No nuts were allowed. Coach Bedard re-wrote a few of them to make them more readable.

Michaela took a quick peek at Belinda's Mohawk Milk Cakes. Alice had made Mini Japanese

Cheesecakes. Jason and Colin had teamed up to create Nanaimo Bars. Coach Bedard offered Butter Tarts with raisins visible in the gooey filling. Some others were Lumberjack Cookies with plaid red and black topping, Newfoundland Snowballs, Maple Cinnamon Rolls, and Coach Mazzocato's Chocolate Dipped Cannoli.

Soon, students and teachers made their selections and paid cashier Coach Bedard. Eventually, crumbs were the only evidence that the baked goods ever existed.

Before returning to classes, Melanie and Hennie approached Michaela.

"This was a great idea, Michaela," Melanie said.

"Yep. I was scared to bake cupcakes, but I'm glad I did," Hennie added.

The $340 raised was to be presented to the Helping Hand Food Drive rep on Friday before the Thanksgiving weekend. All agreed that it was a resounding success. And it had not disrupted their cross-country training schedule, as some had feared.

Michaela had the biggest grin on her face.

She was proud that her idea had been accepted. And how it had been realized and supported by everyone. It was more fulfilling than doing something on her own. *What a cool team and cool school community I'm a part of!* she thought.

10 The INVITATION

It was a warm, breezy afternoon when the Morningside girls' teams arrived at Woodbine Park in the Beaches area of Toronto.

Michaela had attended various summertime festivals there — AFROFEST and the Muhtadi International Drumming Festival. It was like she could still smell the delicious food and hear the sounds of the drums. She had sometimes strolled along the boardwalk with Mom, Dad and Kaffy. She remembered that there was always lots of activity. People played beach volleyball, sunbathed and swam in the water, canoed, kayaked, wind-surfed, jogged and walked their dogs. This time she was there for a different reason. But she still missed Kaffy's company.

They found their school number at Tent City and settled in.

"Keep off the sand so you don't get any in your shoes before the race," Coach Bedard advised.

As they warmed-up along the boardwalk, Michaela

quickly got used to the springy bounce it offered. The sun was high in the sky. The water was rough and uninviting.

"It's so windy," Alice said. She covered her face with her hand.

Michaela wondered why Alice was complaining.

"That's why Coach asked us to bring sunglasses," Belinda said. "The wind and the glare off the water here are different from at Thompson Memorial Park."

"Cross-country running isn't for wimps. You have to adjust to all conditions and surfaces," Melanie said to no one in particular.

But it was clear that she meant Alice, who quickly fished her sunglasses out of a pocket and slipped them on.

"Don't look so worried, Michaela, you'll be fine," Melanie said, giving her a quick hug.

Back in their tent, Coach Bedard gathered them for final instruction. "The course will be altered slightly between races. So there are no secrets the Grade Sevens can pass on. Keep your competitive spirit and have fun."

A whistle was blown instead of a starter's pistol. Michaela and the team watched the Grade Sevens blast off, then went back to their stretching. Their race would be minutes after the last runner came in. Michaela was excited to try something new.

The Grade Eight runners started on grass facing east. Soon, Michaela felt asphalt under her running shoes.

They were on the bike trail, running two or three

across. It was hard to pass. *Hang in there, Michaela*, she told herself.

They turned left and were back on grass. The girls crawled up an incline, north towards Queen Street. As they ran along Queen, Michaela knew where they were when they passed the Kew Gardens Gazebo. Bands played there during the Beaches International Jazz Festival. Heading south again with the public library to her left, Michaela passed a couple of runners. They crossed the bike trail and stomped onto the boardwalk and turned left, heading east once more. All she could hear was thirty-five pairs of running shoes on boards.

We definitely sound like a stampede, she thought. *A buffalo stampede this time, not bulls.* Again she wished she had someone to share the thought with.

But the wind was at her back and she was running great. Ahead in the distance, Michaela could see the front runners. Belinda was there, so tall her head was above the others.

The front runners had turned at the sign reading "*Balmy Beach Club*" and were running back along the sand.

Michaela could see that Hennie was ahead of Melanie. Michaela jumped down into sand. Soft sand. They were running into the wind. Behind her, Alice was heading towards the turn. The runners in front of her were spread out and seemed to be having the same sand challenges. No one was passing at this point.

I might as well be running in Jell-O, she thought.

Then thoughts turned to Dad. She had not seen him by the time her race started. Had he made it? Had his job interview delayed him?

She decided to concentrate on her race. She had seen runners at the Grade Seven finish line, on the boardwalk.

Will the rest of our race be on sand? she wondered. *How will I have a chance to move up?*

When she hopped back onto the boardwalk near Leuty Lighthouse, she decided to sprint. This was blind running. She felt a new reserve of energy. She picked off runners one by one while fighting against the wind. Others must have sensed the finish line, just like she did. She was suddenly in a faster sprint with three girls.

Loud voices were cheering. Michaela increased her stride like she was at the end of a 400, not a 3-K. She flew across the finish line.

Suddenly Michaela was sliding across sand scattered across the boardwalk. She pitched forward. Her upper body stopped and her face, without her sunglasses, felt warm against the boards.

She heard voices around her.

"Help her up."

"Hey, are you okay?"

"Don't move her yet."

"Get the medic."

"Michaela, Dad's here."

"Did she hit her head? She could have a concussion."

Michaela blinked and rolled onto her back. She saw Dad and smiled. As she pushed with her hands and sat up, she saw blood around her knee. It was oozing out of a long gash.

"How do you feel, sweetheart?" Dad raised her up onto her right leg.

Another voice. "I'm her coach, Cecile Bedard."

"Michael. Michael Robinson," Dad introduced himself.

"Can you walk to that bench, Michaela?" Coach Bedard asked.

Michaela nodded and made it to the bench with Dad's support. She sat down as the medic arrived and opened her kit.

"Did you hit your head?" the medic asked.

"No, my knee," Michaela said. "I fell forward. Face-planted." She laughed.

The medic started to clean the wound on her knee.

"Owww," Michaela winced. "Did I cross the finish line?"

"You don't remember? You tumbled right after crossing it," Belinda replied.

"That's a deep cut. It's beginning to swell," the medic said as she put on a bandage. "You'll probably need stitches."

"I'll take her to the hospital," Dad said.

11 No CONCUSSION

Michaela called Mom when they were on the way to the hospital. She convinced her mom not to leave work by promising to keep her informed.

The emergency department at Centenary Hospital was not very busy when Michaela and Dad arrived. Michaela had not been here since she was eight years old and had broken her arm. She felt a connection to the building. It was where she had been born and where her grandma had died.

They checked in and were processed by a nurse who checked her vitals — weight, height, blood pressure, temperature, pulse and heart rate. Blood was drawn. An ID band was taped around her wrist. Michaela did not mind the needles that quickly went in and out of her body. But she was not looking forward to the stitches.

There was some waiting.

In the X-ray department, a technician took several pictures of Michaela's knee, thigh and leg.

More waiting. More tests.

Back in the ER, Michaela was given a cubicle. She sat on the bed and texted Mom.

Waiting to meet with a doctor. Wearing two designer gowns — one opened at the front, one opened at the back. Not ironed. Many strings. Previously worn by thousands.

She added a selfie with a goofy face.

Dad took the chair beside her. "Here's some juice and a sandwich," he said, handing them over.

"Thanks, Dad. But I'm not spending the night here." She tore into the sandwich.

A second nurse wheeled in a cart. She asked Michaela's name and date of birth to check against her wristband and her chart. Michaela squeezed Dad's hand as the nurse stuck a needle near her knee and sewed up the wound, then wrapped the area with a non-stick bandage.

"Here are the instructions to keep the stitches clean." The nurse handed Dad two pages.

Much more waiting for the doctor to come.

"The X-rays were clean. No broken bones or fractures," Dr. Grossman said.

"I'm running cross-country," Michaela said.

"Not for a while," Dr. Grossman warned.

"I have a race next Thursday," she pleaded.

"I'd like you to come back on Monday, so I can see how the wound is healing with the stitches. You don't want to reopen that cut. I'll let you know then."

"Why did someone ask about a concussion? I didn't hit my head."

Dr. Grossman looked at her warmly. "No concussion. You've been thoroughly checked. You'll be fine."

Yeah. But how soon can I run? she wondered.

★★★

Michaela met with Coach Bedard in her office before the Friday team meeting started. She told her about the ER visit.

"No concussion?"

"No."

"It's a serious cut on your leg, though. You won't be able to run for several days. I'm moving Alice up to the fourth position. I can't see how you can run in the Northeast Conference Finals. Michaela, I'm sorry. You're off the team."

"I'm using an ice pack. The swelling's going down," she argued. "Please don't kick me off the team, Coach."

"You limped in here, still in pain. You can't train with those stitches." Coach Bedard was silent for a moment. Then she said, "I'll hold the alternate spot until you see the doctor again."

"Can I sit in on the team meeting?" *Please say yes*, she hoped.

"All right. Here's your participation ribbon from the race. You placed ninth. Pretty good. You girls were second. Here's another ribbon. Congratulations."

"Thanks, Coach." It was her first top-ten finish! Out of only thirty-five. "And Alice?" she asked curiously.

"Fourteenth."

Ten minutes later Michaela entered the classroom for the team meeting.

"Michaela, I heard you were in the hospital with a concussion. How come you're at school?" Melanie asked.

"It's only a cut. Who told you I had a concussion?"

"I saw it on Facebook," Hennie said.

"People think you're in some kind of coma," Jason added.

"That's a lie," Michaela said. Where did that rumour come from?

Coach Bedard entered with Belinda and announced her decision about Michaela. Her teammates' reactions were swift.

"The season's over," Melanie groaned.

"We'll never make City Finals now," Hennie added.

"I'll practise harder, guys, I promise," Alice said to reassure them.

"We don't have enough time," Melanie sneered. She shot a look at Michaela.

"Don't blame Michaela. Anyone could fall or not finish a race," Belinda reasoned.

"Well, I didn't," Melanie spat.

"You're pissed off because Hennie beat you," Belinda said. "Grow up."

"I can't see why you're standing up for Michaela, *captain*," Melanie yelled. "She's the one who couldn't keep her balance and spoiled our chances."

"Enough!" Coach Bedard raised her voice. "You're supposed to be a team helping each other. Not picking each other apart. Celebrate the fact that, as a team, you got second place ribbons. An achievement that Michaela, here, contributed to."

There was silence.

"We have six days," Belinda said. "We're a team."

We're not acting like one, Michaela thought. She felt hurt by all the blame.

"Any questions?" Coach Bedard asked.

"What can we do about side stitches," Jason asked. He clearly wanted to distract from the drama. "I get them sometimes during a long run, but not in a race."

"Stop laughing, then," Melanie smirked.

A few of them tittered.

"That's an important question," Coach Bedard said. "It's been thought to be a muscle spasm of the diaphragm. And the diaphragm muscle is significant for your breathing." She looked around. "It can happen to anyone at any time. I've had them. Sharp pains."

"So, there's nothing to do but stop and wait?" Alice asked.

"You might stop, depending on how severe it is. Bend from your waist and get your breathing back to an even rhythm with slow deep breaths. Continue running when you can. I've known some people to run through a stitch," Coach Bedard replied.

"Is there anything to prevent them from happening?" Alice asked. "Especially on race day?"

"Watch your sugar intake." Coach Bedard advised. "Have a lighter breakfast. Be aware of your breathing rhythm. If you're suddenly taking lots of shallow breaths and tensing up your body, that could trigger it. The general aim, as I've said before, is to run as relaxed as possible. Even when sprinting. I know that's not easy, but it will come with more experience."

She got up and went over to her laptop that was hooked to the SMART Board. Then she added, "Hey, most of you may never get one. I want you to be aware, though."

She signalled to Belinda, who switched off the overhead lights. "This is a two-minute clip of senior high school girls in the middle of a cross-country race," she explained. "Watch how they're breathing."

When it was over, she ran another clip. It was of high school boys.

"Notice, in addition to breathing, how relaxed their bodies are overall."

She switched off the interactive whiteboard.

"Let's do some deep breathing exercises. Close your eyes . . ."

***

Michaela limped into homeroom. Her classmates were chatting among themselves. A few of them turned and looked at her. There was what she thought was a mixture of surprise and pity in their eyes. Mr. Riley looked up from his desk with his eyes bulging.

"Should you be at school, Michaela?" he asked. "I heard you had a concussion."

"No concussion," she said sternly, loud enough for everyone to hear. "Just a cut across my knee."

The morning bell sounded.

During lunch period Michaela sat by herself in the cafeteria. She felt like a flu virus victim. She was still shocked from being kicked off the team. Her smartphone pinged with an incoming text. Belinda.

meet me out back

Moments later, she joined Belinda and listened as the team captain explained her plan.

12 Smells Bad, DOES THE JOB

Michaela left home on Saturday afternoon and slowly walked east on Ellesmere. She had iced her knee that morning and the evening before. The area sill felt tight, but there was no pain.

If I had to fall, why couldn't it be next month instead? she wondered hopelessly.

Michaela knew that it was no good beating herself up. She checked the numbers on the large houses she had always noticed on her way to the library. Farther along, she crossed to the south side and spotted the blue Tesla beside a red one in the carport.

Belinda came out to greet Michaela before she rang the doorbell. She led Michaela down to the basement, carrying her running shoes. The room was huge, with high ceilings and large windows. They passed a half-dozen round leather items with animal artwork and patterns hooked along a wall. Michaela paused to admire them.

"Hand drums," Belinda said. She unhooked one and took it down.

"You play?"

"We all play. Well, mainly me and my older brother. At powwows."

She handed the drum to Michaela, who examined the one-sided drum and the pattern on the skin. She had never held one before. Michaela had seen ads for the Annual Indigenous Festival with dancers, drummers and singers, but never had a chance to attend.

"It's light."

"Not after the first hour of playing."

"We're both drummers, then. I play the steel drum. It's made from —"

"Oil drums. The only musical instrument invented in the twentieth century. From Trinidad and Tobago. You can play, let's see, calypso, soca, jazz. Latin, classical, Pop . . . anything on it. You're lucky you don't have to hold it in your hand. Yours hooks onto a stand. And I've been to Caribana, or whatever they decide to call it now . . ."

"Stop, stop," Michaela laughed. "I get it, you know the culture."

They settled in an exercise area. Michaela noticed a massage table, a stationary bicycle, a treadmill, a rack with free weights and exercise mats.

"Take off your sweatpants," instructed Belinda. "Hop onto the massage table and lie down like a good patient."

"Yes, captain," Michaela said.

Belinda washed and dried her hands. She removed the dressing on Michaela's knee and placed it beside her. Then she unscrewed a jar full of a dark substance. She scooped some out with two fingers and spread it over and around the stitches.

Michaela scrunched up her nose.

"Yes, it smells bad, but it does the job," Belinda said. She held the jar beside her face like she was in a commercial.

"What's in it?"

"Bushes, herbs. This one might have some bear grease. It's one of my grandmother's secret medicines. An ointment. She has promised to teach me to make stuff like this when I'm older."

"It's kinda warm . . . almost burning."

"It's doing the job," Belinda said. She kept massaging the stuff onto Michaela's knee.

"Feels good." Michaela yawned. She stretched her arms behind her head and pretended to fall asleep.

"No chance," Belinda said. "Treadmill time. That is, if you still want to run next Thursday."

"You got that right."

Belinda bandaged the knee. Michaela sat up and slowly eased off the massage table. She tied her running shoes and stepped onto the treadmill.

"Hold on tight," Belinda warned, as she set the program on the screen. "You're starting slowly. Any discomfort, tell me and I'll stop it."

Belinda placed a hand on the small of Michaela's back to support her. After the first two minutes, Michaela got used to the treadmill. "I can walk faster," she said.

Belinda removed her hand. "This is an exercise, not a race. I don't want you to pop those stitches. Then I'd lose my medical license."

"You planning on being a real doctor?"

"Maybe. Traditional and alternative combined. In six years I hope to qualify as an Olympian."

"Marathon?"

"I'm thinking 5-K and 10-K. I'm not sure I have the patience for the marathon. My dad ran a few marathons."

"Does your brother run too?

"No. Plays lacrosse. He's away at Queen's University. Mom's specialty was soccer. What are your plans?"

"I want to have my own all-female steel band orchestra. Take it on tour. Play all kinds of music." Michaela went on to tell Belinda about her parents until the treadmill stopped.

"Twenty minutes," Belinda announced. "How do you feel?"

"Pretty good."

They took a break and sat on the sofa, sipping juice.

"With a fall like that, some girls would have called it a season," Belinda said. "Why are you running cross-country, Michaela?"

Michaela was surprised by the question. No one had asked her that before. She didn't want to talk about the girls at summer camp. She didn't know how Belinda, a serious runner, would judge her for running because others thought she shouldn't. But then something came to mind that was a truth.

"When I ran track, last spring, I was the only one doing the 400. The other girls were doing the 100 and 200 and the relay. It was lonely. I didn't really feel part of the team."

"Have you felt part of our team?"

"Sometimes. The overall goal has been team results. I get along with Melanie and Hennie. We're not buddies, though. Alice is . . . ahh . . . polite."

"I've tried to make Alice feel part of the team."

"I see that. And you've been helpful to me all along. A real leader."

"Thanks, Michaela. Keep in mind that, with cross-country, things can change. A runner can have a good race or a poor one, even if they're in good condition."

"Coach says aim to better our best and see what happens," Michaela said.

"I want you to be able to run on Thursday. Even if you jog the whole race. You're my teammate."

Michaela felt a boost. Thursday was possible, after all. She wondered why Belinda didn't say anything about Melanie and Hennie's behaviour when Coach dropped her from fourth.

Then she realized that Belinda's silence was show-ing wise leadership. *I'm lucky she's our captain*, Michaela thought. *And maybe my friend, too.*

★★★

"What's that smell?" Mom asked.

Michaela told her about the ointment and showed her the small jar. Belinda had given her instructions to apply it twice more before she went to bed.

Mom unscrewed the jar and sniffed. "Lord, child, I'm going to burn some incense." She fetched some coconut oil and handed it to Michaela. "Add this to it. Or your poor father and I won't get a minute of sleep tonight."

Michaela decided not to tell her mom about the treadmill.

A few hours later she lay in bed thinking about the day. It had been the first time she felt comfortable talking with another girl since Kaffy moved away. She knew that it was hard for her to make friends. And she promised herself that she would make a better effort in the future.

13 Fast HEALER

As agreed, Michaela returned to Belinda's basement on Sunday morning.

"Here's some cornbread," Michaela said, handing Belinda a large plastic container. "Dad's recipe from the American South."

"I thought your dad was Trini."

"No, that's my mom. Although Dad sounds that way sometimes. He's originally from Brooklyn with deep roots in Texas."

"How did your parents meet?"

"He came up one Caribana weekend, met mom and moved here. Careful, it's got jalapeno peppers. I hope you like hot."

"I like hot and spicy," Belinda said, taking out one of the small squares.

"Save some for your folks."

"Good idea," she said as she took a bite. "Very nice. Moist, too. We'll munch in the car."

"In the car?"

"We're driving to Kingston later to have Thanksgiving with my brother."

"Let's not waste any more time, then," Michaela said.

***

Monday was Thanksgiving Day. Some years the Robinsons hosted a dinner. Other times they visited relatives or friends outside of Toronto. This year's plans had changed with Michaela's accident. They enjoyed a quiet, simple, baked turkey lunch with freshly stewed cranberries, American sweet potato pie, Brussels sprouts, and Trinidadian callaloo with okras.

"Ah, Thanksgiving number one," Dad smiled. "One more to go." Because of Dad's background, the family also celebrated American Thanksgiving in November. Michaela was proud of all her heritage celebrations.

Michaela suggested that they hold off on the apple-peach crumble pie and soursop ice cream until they returned from the hospital. Mom and Dad raised their eyebrows in surprise and agreed before she changed her mind. Before leaving, Mom advised Michaela to wipe off all traces of the ointment she had applied after her morning shower. Mom wrapped her clean knee with a fresh bandage.

It was Michaela's idea to walk off their meal up the long hill on the west side of Ellesmere. This would be Michaela's only exercise for the day. Mom agreed, on the condition that they stop for her favourite Tim Hortons drink on the way back.

In the outpatient area of the hospital, a nurse paged Dr. Grossman and escorted them to an exam room. Michaela wore a nice pair of shorts. She hoped that, with her knee exposed, she could avoid the awful hospital gowns. She hopped up onto the padded table, ready.

In no time Dr. Grossman arrived. "Hello, Robinson family," he said, closing the door behind him.

Michaela wasted no time. "I'm ready to run, Dr. Grossman."

"Let's have a look at that knee first." He placed her chart on a small desk and pulled on a pair of latex gloves. "Please swing your legs up."

As Michaela leaned back onto her elbows, he removed the bandage.

"The swelling's gone, as expected. No discolouration. Wow! Healthy tissue. Is this the same knee? Did you get a new knee somewhere?" he teased.

"I switched with my mom," Michaela fired back.

"When's the Netflix stand-up special coming?" he asked Mom and Dad.

They smiled politely.

He poked at the wound and the area around it. "No pain?"

Michaela shook her head.

He opened the door and called out, "Conchita."

Seconds later, Nurse Conchita wheeled in a cart with instruments.

"Looks like we're removing stitches, Conchita," Dr. Grossman said.

"Yes!" Michaela clapped her hands.

Nurse Conchita pulled on latex gloves and cleaned the wound with an antiseptic wipe. Using scissors and a pair of tweezers, she removed the stitches. She applied another wipe and washed the knee with antibacterial soap. She then dried it and wrapped a fresh bandage before wheeling out the cart.

"Clean," Dr. Grossman said. "You're a fast healer."

"The genes, doc, the genes," Dad boasted.

Michaela and Mom exchanged a look. They knew differently. It was the ointment.

"No stiffness?" Dr. Grossman asked.

"None at all," said Michaela firmly. "I feel . . . normal. Can I run Thursday, Dr. Grossman?"

"I don't see why not. Keep it bandaged when exercising, especially when you're in the sun. What do you say, Mom and Dad?"

"Fine with us," Mom spoke up.

"I'll need a note for my cross-country coach. Please," Michaela added.

Dr. Grossman wrote the note and handed it to Mom. "Don't take this the wrong way, Michaela. I hope I never see you in here again."

No, way, doc, she thought. *Now I can try to help my team.*

14 Welcome BACK

The early mornings were colder now. Summer was in deep sleep. Fall was wide awake. The leaves had deeper hues of gold, crimson and red when they fell. Michaela biked to school extra early on Tuesday morning. She waited anxiously outside Coach Bedard's office.

"Good morning, Michaela," said Coach Bedard when she arrived.

"Good morning, Coach," Michaela responded, waving two sheets of paper. "It *is* a good morning."

Coach Bedard unlocked the door and switched on the lights. She gestured for Michaela to sit. As she did, Michaela handed over the papers. Dr. Grossman's note and one from Mom and Dad giving parental permission.

Coach Bedard read, nodding. "Show me your knee."

Michaela unwrapped the bandage. "This is mainly for sun protection," Michaela explained.

"That healed fast. No more stitches," Coach Bedard said, surprised. "I know how much you're enjoying cross-country, Michaela. I'm putting you back as the alternate. You've lost some training time, but your presence will help the others. After all, you did help the team get to the Northeast Conference Finals."

"Thanks, Coach," she beamed.

"Take your time with stretching and warm-up."

Michaela did not mention the treadmill. Or the ointment, which she planned to keep applying throughout the week.

Her teammates, including the boys, welcomed her back. Belinda hugged her like they had not seen each other in a long time.

"Thanks, again," Michaela whispered to her.

"Any time," Belinda whispered back. "You smell like coconut."

"It's my new body wash." Michaela dared not reveal to Belinda that she had added coconut oil to grandmother's prized ointment.

Michaela was careful not to run too hard during the morning practices and the afternoon speed work. She had also decided not to show that she was competing with Alice, so she lagged behind her. She knew that she was not yet back to her top speed and conditioning. And Alice appeared to run with more confidence than before.

★★★

Rain had pelted down that Thursday morning. But no practice was scheduled, so there was no time lost. It was overcast with no sun peeking through the clouds to brighten the afternoon. The grass was still wet.

Michaela re-read a text from Dad:

Alternate? Doesn't matter. You're a team member. Help your team.

The Northeast Conference Finals at Thompson Memorial Park felt strange to Michaela. She did not feel the pressure she felt before to hold the team up. Yet, she wondered if she was strong enough to beat Alice and give the team more support. Only the first four teams would advance to the City Finals. They needed all the good times they could get.

From the warm-up, Michaela knew that parts of the course were slippery. She would have to be careful. She double-checked that the bandage was secure. She was here to compete. This was not going to be a long jog like the ones she took with Dad. She missed Dad, but he had a meeting about a weekend course.

Once more, Michaela positioned herself in the middle of the pack. Except that, this time, she was behind Alice. On purpose. This time, Michaela was doing the chasing.

The flag was lowered.

The start was faster than the qualifier. Even though

Michaela knew the course, she struggled to keep up.

At one point, two girls ahead of her slipped and crashed. She avoided a collision. Her race goals became: *One: I will not fall. Two: I will finish this race, no matter what.*

Her knee felt fine. Near the end of the first loop the course curved. That's where she got a proper look at the runners stretched out ahead. Alice was way in the distance. That meant Belinda, Melanie and Hennie were even farther along. Michaela was running even slower than she had imagined.

She wondered if it might be their last race for the season. The thought jolted her. She sprinted through two open areas, passing runners. Then she slowed down when the course narrowed. Halfway through the last loop Alice's red headband was in clear sight.

She set a new goal: *Aim to keep up with Alice.*

With about 600 metres to go, Alice looked back twice, searching. Her eyes locked onto Michaela's. Alice appeared to have a surge of energy as she passed other runners.

Keep up, Michaela, she told herself.

Michaela started sprinting also. But earlier than she had planned. Alice looked back once more to see Michaela gaining ground. Alice looked frightened, like she was being chased by a tiger. Michaela crossed the finish line and entered the funnel four runners behind Alice. She had given her best and finished. She had not fallen.

But Alice had beaten her.

The Morningside Grade Eight girls' team placed fourth. The celebration continued into the Friday morning team meeting. For the first time in years, all four Morningside teams had advanced to the City Finals.

Belinda had placed fourth overall. She confided to Michaela that she intended to do much better. The top five were grouped together. Their times were just seconds apart.

"One more race. Do you have it in you?" asked Coach Bedard.

"Yes, Coach!" they shouted in unison.

"Are you sure, Morningside?"

"Yes, Coach."

"City Finals will be tougher than anything you experienced before. This year it will not be at Centennial Park." Coach Bedard handed out papers. "Here is the High Park course."

"Where's High Park?" Hennie asked.

"In the west end. It's huge." Alice said brightly. "I've been there in May for the Cherry Blossom Festival. Sakura trees. Pink. White. It's so pretty. The blossoms last seven to ten days. You are reminded that life is fragile. And beautiful. And short. It feels like you're in Japan. You guys should go next year."

"Thanks, Alice," Coach Bedard said.

"Cross-country season is short, too. And beautiful," Alice added with bright eyes.

The other girls stared at Alice like she had woken from a deep sleep. Those were the most words she had strung together at once in their presence. Until now, Alice had given no hint that running was so important to her.

The rumour that she had a concussion suddenly popped into Michaela's head. Who would have gained by spreading it? One name came to mind. Alice. Alice moved up from alternate to a member of the team when it looked like Michaela couldn't compete.

Michaela decided to shake off the thought as Melanie brought them back to the subject at hand.

"It looks normal. Other than more trees," she said.

"This course is trickier than it looks," Coach Bedard said. "That's why I've decided to hold a special practice there tomorrow."

There was surprised murmuring.

"Check with your parents. If you can't make it, let me know sometime today."

"How will we get there?" Michaela asked. Dad would be attending a special weekend course and couldn't drive her. Mom was also busy.

"Carpool. This is only for you Grade Eights." Coach Bedard replied.

"What if it rains? It's supposed —" Jason started.

"We run. Rain or shine. Snow or hail. Monsoon or frogs falling from the sky," Coach Bedard stated.

Some of them giggled.

"There's a hill before the finish line. They call it *Zoo Hill*."

"Why do they call it Zoo Hill?" Hennie asked.

"It runs by a tiny zoo that's been there for more than a hundred years," Coach Bedard replied.

She handed out white envelopes with names on the outside saying, "One more thing. These are for your eyes only. Please do not share or discuss with each other. Open your envelope when you are alone."

"What's in it?" Belinda asked.

"An assignment that will take you about half an hour. You have directions for finding the information. It's something I want you to enjoy doing. Then you will share what you've found next Wednesday after school."

The runners looked at each other, confused and curious.

Coach Bedard took them through a visualization exercise of running through a forest.

15 Meeting ZOO HILL

Everyone arrived at the Grenadier Restaurant parking lot at 1:00 p.m. The air was cool and bright. Michaela observed the dense trees and the colourful carpet of leaves that covered the ground. This was a different type of park from Thompson Memorial. It was more alive, with skateboarders, dog walkers, cyclists and joggers.

Belinda and Mr. Troutman had picked up Michaela before collecting Alice. Alice lived in one of the townhouses off Morningside Avenue opposite the Toronto Pan Am Sports Centre. It was a ten minute walk from Michaela's home. Michaela hadn't realized how close Alice lived to her. She was puzzled that she had never seen Alice in her neighbourhood.

Coach Bedard's car contained Melanie, Hennie and Jason. The other four boys came with a mom, Mrs. Choi. After introductions, they all walked over to the starting area for group stretching exercises.

"For the warm-up, we're going to slowly jog what I figure will be the course," Coach Bedard started.

"There are no markers up today. But it will be close enough for you to get a feel for the route."

Everyone was spaced out, solo. The girls first, then the boys, followed by Mr. Troutman and Mrs. Choi.

They started off facing Bloor Street, going north. Before they got to the street they turned right across grass and leaves beside the tennis courts. Then down a small hill to a single track through trees. Turning right, they were going south, up and down small mounds. Michaela soon lost track of directions, but that did not matter. They stopped at a road to allow two cars to pass.

"There will be course marshals and volunteers to stop any vehicles," Coach Bedard explained. "The usual traffic, including trackless trains, will stop at noon on Thursday. Except for tagged vehicles related to the Finals."

Then they were crossing a small bridge over a brook, up a mound, and down again. And across a paved path. They entered a road with a small parking lot on the left. Coach Bedard stopped them outside the lower gate. There was a sign:

Welcome To High Park Zoo

"Girls, boys, meet Zoo Hill. Someone with a sense of humour designed the course to go through the middle of the zoo."

"Yeah, they wanted to throw us off with all the smells," Jason quipped.

They chuckled while Coach Bedard checked her

watch. "By this time, you will have been running for . . . seven minutes, give or take. So you're three or four minutes from the end," Coach Bedard said. "The animals on either side of the road are in safe pens. No way they'll escape and chase you, so don't worry."

The runners pointed out different animals, including llamas, with ducks waddling around their pens. Capybaras. Emus. Bison. Barbary sheep with horns — Michaela thought they looked like goats. Peacocks. And reindeer.

Coach Bedard led them slowly up the long, gradual hill and through the upper gate.

"Here comes the steepest part. Roughly one hundred metres to the top," she stated.

At the top, she stopped and waited for everyone to catch up with her. They were bent over, panting.

"People, it's not over yet," she laughed. "This is where you cannot stop. Over there is the parking lot where we arrived. From here there's about 400 metres to the finish line. You must have a reserve of energy to sprint to that finish line. Let's keep going."

The girls looked at each other. Michaela knew they were all thinking the same thing: *You got to be kidding me!*

"Almost there," Belinda smiled, jogging away.

They stopped at the invisible finish line near the high fencing of the baseball enclosure.

"Anyone need a washroom?" Coach Bedard asked. Hands shot up.

"I'll take you," Mrs. Choi offered and led them away.

When they had re-assembled, Coach Bedard gathered them in a circle.

"How do you feel?" she asked.

"Centennial Park has more open spaces for passing," Jason said.

"And what does this course tell you?"

"You need a strong start," Belinda offered. "And the strongest finish ever. We'll have to put in more speed work next week."

"Exactly," Coach Bedard said, as she led them again in stretches. "We'll go over it again. This time we run. Not for speed, but to get a good feel for the rhythm of the course. No stopping unless we encounter vehicles. Keep your sweats on."

She huddled briefly with Mr. Troutman and Mrs. Choi. Michaela watched them pointing at course maps and looking at their watches.

Coach Bedard led off. Mr. Troutman looked at his watch and sent the boys team seconds later. Michaela checked her own watch.

After two minutes, Mr. Troutman said to the girls' team, "If you need to pass me, go ahead. Mrs. Choi and I will always be close by." Then he took off.

Seconds later, Mrs. Choi sent them off. She trailed behind.

Michaela, once again, stayed last. This was not a race. At the bottom of Zoo Hill, she looked upwards.

The boys were not visible. Her teammates were strung out ahead.

She wanted to stop at the top of the hill. She urged herself forward. Four hundred metres more.

As soon as she crossed the invisible finish line, Michaela bent over. Even Mrs. Choi was breathing hard.

"Walk it out, everyone. Keep moving," Coach Bedard instructed.

"That Zoo Hill's a killer," Melanie blurted out.

"Like a blow to the head," Jason added. He slapped his forehead with both hands in a comedic way.

Everyone laughed, including Michaela. But she noticed Alice mirroring Jason, knocking her head with her hands. And there was something about the way Alice glanced at Michaela right after doing it.

The concussion, Michaela thought. *I bet it was Alice who started that rumour.*

Over at the Grenadier Restaurant parking lot, Coach Bedard handed out bottles of water and juice. Michaela, acting on a gut feeling, nudged Alice away from the others.

"Alice, are you the one who told everyone I had a concussion?" Michaela asked in a low voice.

Alice looked at her with surprise, then turned away. When she turned back, her face and neck were flushed.

"Why would I do that?"

Michaela knew she couldn't prove anything. But

Alice hadn't said she didn't do it. And she didn't seem surprised at Michaela's question. "I guess I'll have to start asking around to find out who started the rumour."

Two cars pulled into the parking lot. The Grade Eight girls' team from Kippendavie Public School hopped out. The Morningside girls recognized them from the Beaches Invitational Meet. Coach Bedard exchanged greetings with their coach. Then she turned her attention back to her runners.

"I want to thank you all for coming out today. Thank you, Mrs. Choi and Mr. Troutman, for your assistance. Make tomorrow your rest day, girls and boys. We have a beautiful week ahead. Remember, only one more race."

They headed home. Michaela and Alice sat in the back seat in silence. Before Mr. Troutman dropped her off, Alice leaned over. She whispered, "It was me. I'm so sorry, Michaela."

Michaela had no answer.

★★★

After supper, Michaela opened her laptop to Skype Kaffy. She had an email.

"Hey, M. So-so week. Busy this evening. Oh, I made it onto the under-14 ice hockey team. We started practising this week. Skype next week. Love you," Kaffy wrote.

Michaela replied, "Congratulations. We made City Finals next week. Love you back."

She closed her laptop and hugged it. She realized that she and her best friend were leading different lives.

Maybe they were beginning to grow up. This thought hit Michaela with a wave of sadness. They had known each other a long time. Now they were separated by 200 kilometres. She would have to run sixty of her cross-country courses in a row to see Kaffy.

Michaela finished her now nightly ritual of rubbing the ointment into both knees. She did not have to heal her knee any more. But she felt it relieved overall muscle soreness. Her phone pinged with a text from Belinda.

Got a plan. Come over tomorrow. 10 a.m.?

Sure. See ya.

Michaela hoped Belinda didn't want to go back to High Park.

16 Close YOUR EYES

Belinda had invited Michaela over, and they were hanging out on Belinda's bed, chatting about the team. Ever since Michaela had found out that Alice started the rumour, it had been bothering her. She wasn't sure she should tell the team about it. But was it okay to keep it secret from the team captain?

She told Belinda about the suspicions that led her to ask Alice. And she described how Alice admitted to doing it. "I'm torn and confused," Michaela ended off.

"You can't let it affect the Finals, running with all kinds of thoughts like that in your head. That's in the past, don't wallow in it," Belinda advised. "You could simply forgive her. It would be the right thing for the team."

"I promise I'll think it over." Michaela was suddenly tired of thinking about it. "So what's the big plan?"

"Right. Time to get serious."

They headed to the basement.

"You cycled over here," said Belinda. "So you're already warmed-up. Hop onto the treadmill." She tapped into the screen.

Michaela tied up her running shoes and followed the instructions.

"Grab the handles," Belinda told her. "Think back to the starting line at High Park yesterday. Close your eyes."

"I'll fall."

"Trust me, Michaela. I'm right here. Listen to my voice."

Michaela knew she already trusted Belinda. As a team captain. As a friend. She closed her eyes.

"Ready . . . go," Belinda said as she started the treadmill.

"It's fast," Michaela said.

"Keep going. You're entering the track to the trees . . ."

At times, the treadmill slowed and the front tilted up. Michaela climbed upwards. Then she was running downwards, accompanied by Belinda's voice. It reminded her of Coach Bedard's visualization exercises. Except that this was physical as well as mental.

"Seven minute mark," said Belinda. "You're entering the lower gate on Zoo Hill. Can you smell the animals?"

Michaela started to giggle.

"Don't open your eyes. You still have lots of energy. This is the easiest hill you've ever climbed."

Michaela grunted, breathing hard.

"Don't tense. Relax. Smile. Make your body light. You're flying up this beautiful hill."

Silence.

"Near the top now," Belinda continued. "When you reach the top you will hear a starter's pistol go off for the 400-metre race you've been warming up for."

This was a warm-up?

"Bang!"

The treadmill sped up. Michaela struggled. But she kept going.

"Imagine, this is your race. Bring it home. See the finish line. Burst through it."

And Michaela did. The treadmill slowed to a walking pace.

"Open your eyes, Michaela. Don't get off yet. Walk it off."

Afterwards, they sat on the sofa drinking cranberry juice.

"That was amazing," marvelled Michaela. "How did you think to create it?"

"I've only used the treadmill for steady pacing. After I got back yesterday, I thought about it. I'd run hills before. Never one that was near the end of a course. I looked at the treadmill and fooled around with some settings. Tried it four times before I was sure it was a good test."

"Four times? You're crazy. Glad you invited me, though."

"What you did was phase one. Are you ready for phase two?"

"There's *more*?"

"Actually, three phases. Phase three, you walk on your hands. All right, only two phases. Phase two is eyes open. And hands-free."

★★★

As Michaela rode her bike home, she realized that she was not as alone as she had thought. It began to drizzle. She made it into her building before the rain got heavy.

"Your dad has some news to share with you," Mom shouted as Michaela opened the door.

"We're increasing the grocery budget for the next five years until you leave home. No new clothes," Dad joked to Michaela. "You're eating too much."

Mom took up the joke. "If we're not careful, Michael, we could end up skin and bone. These runners, as they get older, eat twice their weight at one sitting." She opened her eyes wide.

"Remember the chicken race we saw on our honeymoon?" Dad prompted.

"How could I forget? Eight thirteen-year-old girls each picked up a whole roast chicken with their teeth."

"The same way people bob for apples floating in a barrel of water," Dad said.

"Right. And, *bam*, they ran one hundred metres,

dropping parts of chickens along the track. The tall thin girl won by a neck," Mom deadpanned.

They both cracked up at their story. They high-fived each other for their performance.

Michaela smirked.

"The news — the good news — is that I'm going to set up my own business, from home. As a life coach," Dad announced.

"That's great," Michaela said. "Sounds like what you've been doing as a manager."

"The human resources part, yes. That's why it will take me less time to be certified."

Michaela saw how well suited her dad would be to the job. "You once said that if people don't use their talents and abilities, those gifts from creation wither away. Plus, you've always been giving advice to all kinds of people. You inspired me and helped me try running as part of a team," she said. "How do you feel about this, Mom?" she asked.

"I fully support your dad. He will get to monetize what he's been giving away for free."

Michaela smiled. "So . . . when I'm sixteen I'll be ready for my first paying job at Robinson PLC. Then I'll be thrilled, Mom, for you to negotiate with your wealthy husband to *money-tize* me sixty dollars an hour. Plus benefits."

Mom and Dad looked at her with blank faces.

17 The ELLESMERE

She hears the Olympic stadium crowd of 50,000 erupt as the lead runner enters from the tunnel. She knows there is one lap before the finish line. One hundred and fifty runners started the 42-K marathon. She has been chasing the defending Olympic champion for the last 5-K through the city streets.

She enters the stadium, seconds behind, and the spectators go wild. The sound is deafening, yet strangely musical. It is like being at a soccer and cricket match at the same time. The first time in history that two Canadian females would finish first and second in an Olympic marathon.

She believes with all her being that she can catch the champ. So she finds another gear for a last sprint. She reaches the front runner at the final curve of the track. The spectators scream. She blocks out the sound. They are shoulder to shoulder down the home stretch. With twenty metres to go, she grabs Belinda's hand and lifts it high. They pop the tape together in an unbelievable, photo-finish, double-gold win. They each grab a Canadian flag for their victory lap.

"Michaela . . . Michaela . . ."

She felt a hand shaking her shoulder. She opened her eyes.

I'm . . . in . . . the . . . cafeteria? she realized as she came back to reality.

"Why were you holding your hand high with a half-eaten sandwich?"

"I was not."

"Whatever," Belinda laughed. "I spoke to Coach about your idea. It's a go."

They high-fived. Michaela thought about sharing her daydream. But she held her tongue.

★★★

At practice on Tuesday, Coach Bedard reminded everyone about the white envelope assignment due the next day. Then she led both teams in a jog along the sidewalk on Ellesmere, west to Morningside. They crossed at the traffic lights and stopped at the end of Mornelle Court. Michaela's balcony was visible from there. But these girls and boys were not there to pay a visit to Mom and Dad for Caribbean snacks and guava juice. Michaela's idea was for the teams to run up the long hill she and her parents had walked the week before on the way to the hospital.

She had gained a lot from the treadmill simulation. Yet, she could not see the team taking turns in Belinda's basement. She wanted everyone to benefit together.

They all looked upwards.

"Ladies. Gentlemen. I give you the Ellesmere," Michaela said with a flourish. It was like she was revealing one of Earth's famous mountain peaks. "Coach Bedard will be our Sherpa guide. This promises to be warmer than Mount Everest. No frostbite, I promise."

"Oh my God!"

"Has to be worse than Zoo Hill."

"This is torture."

"Stop your whining," Coach Bedard said. "Run up, jog down slowly. And repeat."

They lined up, ready to conquer the Ellesmere. And they did. Although Michaela heard them muttering curses under their breath.

"Great idea, Michaela," Coach Bedard said as they jogged back to school in a cool-down. "Good of you to think about your teammates' progress."

"Thanks, Coach."

Michaela had been thinking over the rumour thing and Alice. She remembered how determined she had been herself to make the team. How would she feel if someone new made the team and made her alternate? She was starting to see how insecure Alice must have felt to spread the rumour.

She thought about Belinda's advice. Alice had admitted to doing it. She had apologized. Otherwise Michaela would never have found out for sure. She hadn't had any proof.

Michaela needed to do what was best for the good of the team, sooner or later. Before they entered the building, Michaela tugged on Alice's elbow. They stopped to let the others enter.

"Alice, there's something I want to say to you."

Alice cast her eyes to the ground and waited.

Michaela took a breath and said, "I . . . I forgive you."

Alice raised her eyes and sighed with relief. "I really am sorry, Michaela," she said. "It was a stupid thing to do."

Then Alice surprised Michaela by giving her a hug.

Michaela realized she felt relieved from the tension she had been carrying. "No harm done, Alice. You'll get a chance to run a good race as part of the team on Thursday."

Alice looked ashamed. "From the beginning, I told my parents I *was* on the team. I could never have told them I was the alternate."

"Why not?"

"They would have told me to try for another team. Like soccer," Alice replied. "I wanted to run. I know I can do better." She shrugged and entered the school.

Michaela realized how lucky she was that her parents supported her. *Whatever I do*, she thought.

She rushed home and finally opened the white envelope. Right away, she got to work on her assignment.

18 Let Them INSPIRE YOU

"Since this is the eve of your big race, I thought you could use some inspiration," Coach Bedard began. "In these one-minute presentations, you will hear a tiny bit about some Canadian runners who came before you. They are mainly distance runners with a couple of exceptions. Hennie, you're up first."

Hennie stood with a sheet of paper and looked at her fellow runners before reading her report on Toronto-born Jean "Jenny" Thompson, who lived from 1910 to 1976. Michaela was surprised to learn that girls did not run long distances in competition over one hundred years ago. Jenny Thompson won the national title with a world record. Then she finished fourth in the 800-metre at the 1928 Olympics, where women's events were first introduced to the Olympic Games.

"In 1987, she was post . . . posthumously inducted into the Penetanguishene Sports Hall of Fame." Hennie finished and sat down.

Jason stood without a sheet of paper in his hand.

He started to rap.

"Yo, yo, yo.

So, listen up to what I create.

Pioneer John 'Jack' Tait.

1888 to 1971, his dates.

They called Jack the *Boy Wonder*.

You wonder why?

One of the great milers of his era.

That's no error.

Olympian 1908 and 1912.

Fourth best finish, 1,500 metres.

Shook hands with Toronto greeters upon his return.

Rival and close friend of Tom Longboat.

They raced 4-K, 8-K and 24-K marathon.

Proud, confident men, but no showboats.

Jack won gold in the mile at Festival of the Empire Sports.

Thought you'd ask.

No easy task.

The First British Empire Games, London, 1911.

Canadian citizens were in seventh heaven.

Canadian team won the overall championship.

Jack dipped his neck.

King George the Fifth placed both gold medals round.

Who the heck was he you ask?

Grandfather of Queen Elizabeth the Second, I reckon.

Tell you more, with another rhyme —
But . . . I'm . . . outta . . . time."

Jason bowed and sat down to scattered applause.

Alice stood up and raced through her presentation like she could not wait to sit back down. "Pioneer Thomas 'Tom' Longboat, 1887 to 1949. Onondaga distance runner from Six Nations Reserve near Brantford, Ontario. Called the *Bulldog of Britannia*. Won the 1907 Boston Marathon almost five minutes faster than any of the previous ten winners. Competed in the 1908 Olympics in the marathon. Set world records for the 24-K and 32-K races. Inducted into the Canada, Ontario and Indian Halls of Fame. Canada Post issued a stamp honoring him in 2000."

As Michaela listened, she recalled reading a book about Tom Longboat. She hadn't heard of the other runners, not even the one she was assigned. Coach Bedard then pointed to her.

Michaela began: "Ottawa-born, in 1956, and Toronto-raised Paul Williams was the grandson of John 'Jack' Tait who Jason told us about. Paul competed in three Olympics, with a best finish of twenty-first place in the 10-K. He was a four-time national champion in the 5-K.

"Between 1979 and 1992 he held and/or broke Canadian records for the 3-K steeplechase, 3-K indoors and outdoors, regular 5-K and 10-K. He won a bronze medal for 10K at Commonwealth Games and a gold for 5-K in the Goodwill Games. He ran high school cross-country for five years. Guess where, guys?"

When no one guessed quickly enough, she said, "In High Park."

As Michaela sat down, Belinda replaced her. "Lynn Kanuka-Williams was once married to the Paul Williams Michaela just talked about. She was born in 1960 in Regina. She started as a young cross-country runner, like us, and went on to compete in two Olympics. She won a bronze 3-K medal at the 1984 Olympics — the first time that distance was held for women in Olympic history. *Yeah!*

"In 1989 Lynn won a bronze medal at the World Cross Country Championships. She set eleven Canadian running records between 1983 and 1989 in the 1,500-metre, mile, 2-K, 3-K, 5-K and 10-K on the roads. She has been inducted into the Canadian Olympic Hall of Fame."

When it was Melanie's turn she talked about Charmaine Crooks. Melanie told how Charmaine Crooks was born in Jamaica in 1962, and competed for Canada in five Olympic Games. She was 1984 Olympic Silver Medalist in the 4x400-metre relay, and became the first Canadian woman to run 800 metres in under two minutes. She won gold medals at the Pan American, Commonwealth and World Cup Games. In 2006, she was the recipient of the International Olympic Committee Women in Sport Trophy.

Michaela remembered Dad telling her about Charmaine Crooks. He had showed her old videos of her running, so Michaela could observe her style,

Other teammates gave their presentations on past distance Olympians like Silvia Ruegger and Sue French-Lee. And recent Olympian and World Champion Somali-Canadian Mohammed Ahmed, who held the Canadian national record for both 5-K and 10-K.

When all the presentations were done, Coach Bedard stood. "I hope you have been inspired by hearing about just a few outstanding athletes. I encourage you to read more about these and all the other Canadian runners." She passed around photos of each runner in a plastic sleeve with the name on the back.

"Girls and boys, I have a presentation of my own. This runner also set a course record in High Park. Let me introduce you to the Kidd, and I'm not kidding, Dr. Bruce Kidd."

She showed a ten minute, black and white documentary called *Runner*. It showed a young Bruce Kidd training along the boardwalk in the Beaches and competing in a race at East York Collegiate. They sat in awe, seeing greatness in locations where they had run themselves.

When it was over, Coach Bedard told them more about the middle-distance Olympian who won championships in Canada, the USA and Britain.

Michaela was impressed that he became a life-long advocate for the sport, pushing for the removal of sexism and racism within it, embracing diversity. He was the tenth principal at University of Toronto Scarborough, five minutes from their school.

"So are you guys fired up?" asked Coach Bedard.

"Yes, Coach," they screamed together.

Coach Bedard told the teams to get a good night's rest. "Let the memories of their achievements carry you through the course tomorrow," she said.

This brought it all to a head for Michaela.

Diversity. There was that word so many people were using.

She thought back to summer camp. *Rachel, Bethany and Cindy do not know diversity. Not really. They only know their world and how things are supposed to work in it. They look at the city and everyone in it as something different. Something to be rejected, even feared.* Michaela realized that she felt sorry for them.

Alternate or not, Michaela was a part of her team. And she had a new friend in Belinda.

Michaela texted Mom and pleaded for a takeout dinner of spicy vegetable pad Thai with extra peanut sauce. Mom arrived home early and granted her wish. Dad was at a business meeting.

"I'm sorry I can't see you race tomorrow," Mom said between bites.

"No problem, Mom." She hadn't been to see

Michaela run all season.

"Your dad will represent us both."

Michaela twirled the noodles with her chopsticks.

Later on, she settled into bed early, hoping to get a long sleep. But lying in the darkness, she felt her body shaking. She wondered how she could shiver yet not feel cold.

She swung out of bed, pulled on flannel pajamas and climbed back in. She started counting backwards from one hundred while willing herself to drift off. Instead, her mind flashed back to the summer camp cross-country race.

Why am I thinking about this? she wondered.

She saw herself falling on the boardwalk. She was haunted by the idea that she would fall again.

Stop it, Michaela, she told herself. *Don't panic. Admit to yourself you're nervous and your nerves will go away. Nothing bad will happen tomorrow.*

Kaffy's voice came into her head. *"Don't let anybody or anything hold you back."*

She and Kaffy seemed to be drifting apart. But Michaela realized that Kaffy's support had been a part of the whole of her life. It gave her confidence.

She took long, deep breaths and pictured a blue cloudless sky, as Coach Bedard had taught them.

It worked. She went off into a dreamless sleep.

19 City FINALS

Mom, Dad and the Troutmans were in front of Tent City when the teams arrived at High Park.

Michaela greeted them all. "Nice surprise to see you here," she said to Mom.

"I decided that this was important," said Mom. "I'll head back to work afterwards."

"Good luck, sweetheart." Dad kissed Michaela's forehead. He was wearing a cap with *VOLUNTEER* stitched on the front. He called out to Mr. Troutman, who wore a similar cap, and they joined Mrs. Choi and other volunteers.

The atmosphere reminded Michaela of a music festival where everyone was waiting for the music to begin. In this case the music was going to be the sound of feet upon asphalt, grass, packed earth, twigs and leaves, and — when listened for closely — breathing.

Away from Tent City, Belinda led the girls in stretches. The Grade Seven girls' race was soon underway. Jason and the Grade Eight boys would start their warm-up in a while.

Next was the Grade Seven boys' race. Michaela noticed that it went on longer than at Thompson Memorial Park.

"Zoo Hill's beating the heck out of some of them," Belinda whispered to Michaela. "At that point in the race, it's all in the head. Remember what you must do at the top of the hill."

"Raise my arms and wave to all the spectators in a circle," Michaela joked. "Like I've just won a boxing match."

"You're getting worse than my dad." Belinda punched her in the shoulder.

"Oww, my shoulder, how am I gonna run?" Michaela pouted. "Yeah, I remember, Belinda."

Coach Bedard called her teams into a huddle. "Okay, runners, you've prepared for this. I'm proud of you all. Do this for yourselves. And for your teammates. You're getting to do something you love. That's a blessing."

"Thanks, Coach, where's the holy water?" Jason asked, cracking everyone up.

"That's the spirit," Coach Bedard chuckled. She unscrewed her water bottle and sprayed them with it playfully.

They removed their sweats and left them in the care of a parent volunteer. Instead of singlets over regular

T-shirts, each had taken Coach Bedard's advice to wear the singlets over long-sleeved jerseys. It was quite cool. Coach Bedard checked that race numbers were pinned securely to their singlets. No numbers on the backs of hands for this race.

"Your laces," Alice pointed. She bent down in front of Michaela and tied her running-shoe laces. "Tight enough?" she asked, looking up.

"Feels good," Michaela responded. "Thanks, Alice."

"I'm following this month's word — *Kindness*. You were kind enough to forgive me." Michaela was surprised to find she felt it was better that Alice be on the team. It clearly meant so much to her.

There were suddenly three shrill blows on a whistle. It was the last signal to assemble.

Michaela was among the top one hundred Grade Eight Toronto girls' cross-country runners. They shuffled to the starting line on the road. Alice moved closer to the top third of runners. Michaela followed close behind. She looked to her left and right and counted about eight across. No middle-of-the-pack this time. She glanced at her watch. She listened.

Bang! The starter's pistol echoed.

Michaela kept free and clear of any jostling. Off the road, they turned right onto grass alongside the tennis courts. They headed down the single track, a little bunched up.

I don't have my own rhythm yet, thought Michaela. *But I'm not going to panic.*

Next, they were stretched out a bit. Michaela looked at her running shoes and where she was stepping. There were lots of leaves on the ground, much more than last Saturday.

Don't slip, Michaela.

The trail narrowed as they climbed up a mound, and down. Sunlight streamed through the trees. She glimpsed the beauty around her in a flash. Then she thought back to Belinda's treadmill on Sunday. Belinda's voice was calm and strong, guiding her. Except this was the real course, not the simulation.

The earth had a nice bounce. The smell was pungent and pleasant at the same time. Michaela became aware of her breathing. It had settled from the fast pace seconds ago. Or was it minutes ago? She could not tell. She decided not to look at her watch.

They came to a clearing and crossed a road. She noticed two volunteers and a course marshall. Runners zipped past her.

That's okay, there's still time. I'll keep my pace.

They crossed the tiny bridge over a brook.

If this is close to Saturday's practice run, I'm almost at the halfway mark.

She could not see Alice. But Michaela knew that she hadn't passed her. She lengthened her stride and passed two runners. And two more.

A group of five runners passed her before the next clearing. She sped up and passed other runners who had started too quickly. She kept up, steps behind those five runners.

A volunteer stood pointing.

The runners were now two abreast on a path.

Birds chirping. Mom's here. Dad, too. I don't see them — yet.

She suddenly thought of Belinda, somewhere ahead. She hoped her friend was having a good race. Top three was her goal. Michaela allowed a smile onto her face as a yellow leaf floated down in front of her.

She focused on the group of five girls directly ahead of her as pace targets. She passed three more runners. They headed across a long slope, slightly downhill. It was paved. She thought it could be one of the routes for the trackless train that took tourists through the park.

Six runners bounded past her and formed a tight group with the pace targets. A road was ahead. Two volunteers. One volunteer she loved very much held a sign with an arrow pointing to her right. He had a grin on his face that she had seen since she was born.

"You're doing great, sweetheart," Dad shouted as she got closer. "Keep going."

She managed a slight wave and turned right, knowing where she was without looking up. The bottom of Zoo Hill.

She entered the lower gate, not bothering to look

at her watch. She wanted to pass as many girls as possible. And she wanted to reach Alice.

Belinda's voice was strong in her head. *"You still have lots of energy. This is the easiest hill you've ever climbed."*

Michaela extended her stride. She ignored the animals on either side, and passed four of the five runners she was tracking earlier. Seconds later, she raised her head and looked up. Alice's red headband bobbed slowly in her view. Michaela was just three runners from Alice.

Michaela ran alongside Alice. She looked over and saw struggle in Alice's face. And surprise. Halfway up the hill, they both looked to the left. What they saw shocked them.

Hennie.

Hennie was bent over and was holding her side. A course marshall rested a hand on her back.

"A side stitch?" Alice asked.

Michaela nodded. They both realized what this meant for the team. It was up to the two of them. If Michaela finished ahead of Hennie, her points would count for the team, even though she was the alternate. Knowing that Hennie was taken care of, she whispered to Alice, "Let's do this."

Alice nodded. Together, they increased their pace up the hill.

Belinda's voice again came into Michaela's head. *"Make your body light. You're flying up this beautiful hill."*

City Finals

Side by side, Michaela and Alice flew through the upper gate. They passed runners who were dying on the last stretch of Zoo Hill.

Not me, thought Michaela. *Not today.*

She saw Mr. Troutman at the top. His sign pointed to the right of Grenadier Restaurant. He gave her a thumbs up. She managed a quick nod. As she crossed the road to the field, she listened for the sound of the starter's pistol Belinda was about to make go off in her head.

She did not hear it. She was distracted. She looked back to see that Alice had stopped. She was bent over.

20 For the TEAM

Without thinking, Michaela stopped where Alice stood.

"You can't . . . stop . . . here . . . Alice," Michaela panted. If Alice didn't finish, then Hennie's time would count in the team's result. "I got you. Let's go." She grabbed Alice's arm and raised her up. A few runners passed by them. "We're almost there. Take a deep breath."

Michaela looked back. Two runners at the crest of the hill seemed ready to pass out. She turned back to Alice.

"You . . . go." Alice gestured with a shooing motion.

"Keep your eyes on me. Just pretend . . . pretend you're chasing me. Sprint."

Alice took two more deep breaths. "Okay . . . okay . . ."

"Bang!" Michaela said in her head. Instead of Belinda, it was Michaela who fired a starter's pistol in her head to get herself going. She sprinted up a slight incline to the right of Grenadier Restaurant and the

field opened to her.

This is my 400-metre race, she thought.

She was aware of Alice right behind her. She heard her puffing. She saw their Grade Sevens waving and yelling. They zipped past a few runners.

One hundred metres.

She passed more runners. Glancing to her right, she saw Alice near her shoulder.

Knowing that Alice would finish, Michaela powered her legs into one final gear. She flew past two runners and crossed the line.

Where's Alice? she wondered, almost panicked.

Alice was three runners behind her. They kept their spots in the funnel, huffing. Michaela reached back and touched palms with her teammate.

It was the best 400 metres Michaela had ever run.

★★★

Belinda and Melanie greeted Michaela and Alice with high-fives.

"Where's Hennie?" Belinda asked, looking around.

"We passed her on Zoo Hill. She didn't look well." Michaela said.

"Here she comes," Melanie shouted.

Hennie crossed the line. Away from the funnel, they all embraced in a circle.

Coach Bedard joined them. "Good job, girls,"

"You okay, Hennie?"

"Yep. Glad I finished."

But Michaela saw the disappointment in Hennie's eyes.

"Let's get your sweats and go support the boys," Coach Bedard suggested.

As they hurried towards their tent, Belinda whispered to Michaela, "I came fourth. And I'm fine with it."

"I'm happy for you. You worked so hard." Michaela hugged her.

"Listen, I've been thinking about joining a running club in Scarborough. For the indoor winter season."

"Sounds like a good plan towards your Olympic dream."

"I was wondering if you wanted to join."

"Oh. I start steel band classes again next Saturday."

"I don't know the schedule yet. It's only an idea. If you can do both, would you think about it? We'd run the 1,500. You've got great speed. I thought it might be something we could do together. As friends."

"I'll think about it." *As friends*, thought Michaela.

21 Like GOLD

By the time Michaela and Mom returned from the washroom, the awards ceremony was underway.

Coach Mazzocato's Grade Seven girls' team placed fifth. The boys, seventh.

"And continuing with the Grade Eight girls," the race director announced. "Fifth place ribbon: Jennifer Chen from Kippendavie Public School. Fourth place ribbon: Sheila McCrimmon from Cummer Senior Public School."

Michaela looked around for Belinda. The race director had to be mistaken. She had the standings wrong.

"Third place bronze medal: Marva Warner from Grandravine Public School."

Where was Coach? She needed to correct the race director.

"Second place silver medal: Silvana Maria Falsaperla from Rathburn Public School."

Michaela spotted Belinda near the front. She waved to get her attention.

"And our girls' Grade Eight cross-country, gold medal champion this year is Belinda Troutman from Morningside Senior Public School."

To the sound of loud cheers, Michaela thought, *She tricked me!* She was really happy for her new friend.

"Now for our presentations to the Grade Eight girls' teams."

The only thing Michaela heard and would remember for years to come was —

"Third place bronze medals to Morningside Senior Public School."

Because that bronze medal felt like *gold*.

Coach Bedard gathered the Grade Eights once more before they got on the bus. Jason had placed third. And the boys were sixth overall.

"Way to go, girls, boys," Coach Bedard began. "I want to thank you for all your efforts this season. Each of you improved your times. You put in the hard work every week. And you will only get better if cross-country running continues to be a passion as you move into high school next year."

She continued. "Hennie, I know you didn't have the finish you wanted. Or deserved. But, guys, all kinds of things happen in a race. You have the experience, and you move on. Some runners did not make it up Zoo Hill. Some did not even finish. You, Hennie, finished. True, your points did not count in the end. But you contributed at each key race in the season to get your teammates to the Finals. You have a bronze medal. You should feel good about that."

"I will, Coach," Hennie said.

Melanie, standing beside Hennie, placed an arm around her.

"Belinda, Jason," Coach Bedard addressed them. "You have both been solid captains. You've shown leadership with your teams and your part in this is to be applauded."

The others clapped.

"Michaela, Alice told me what you did," Coach Bedard said. She recounted for everyone how Michaela urged Alice on to their finish. "That's a strong example of teamwork, guys. Pizza party at my place on Saturday."

As Michaela went to board the school bus, she thought about the four goals she had set herself when she decided to run cross-country. She had made the team, finished all races and placed eleventh — just outside her top-ten aim. She guessed she could have met that goal, too, if she hadn't stopped to help Alice. So she had not let her teammates down, after all.

She thought of the quote stenciled on Coach Bedard's wall, *"You Form Your Own Destiny From Within Yourself."*

Have I formed my own destiny with all my might? Michaela wondered. With help, she had participated. She was dedicated. She did not give up.

"My spirit is strong," she whispered aloud. "Because it's the spirit of my team."

ACKNOWLEDGEMENTS

I would like to acknowledge the dedication and wizardry of my editor, Kat Mototsune. This is our third book together and I am thankful for her insights and championing of my work.

As always, a big cheer to Carrie Gleason for her support and belief in this project, and to Team Lorimer. Thank you, all.

Thanks to Verna-Marie Hafner, North Cross Country Co-Convenor within the Toronto District School Board for her consulting enthusiasm and technical assistance.

Thanks to my early coaches at Riverdale Collegiate for nurturing in me perseverance, which has extended beyond the autumnal cross-country courses and trails: Dr. Randy Cross, Mr. Robert Breakey and Mr. George Salter.

Blessings upon: Queen Ainajugoh Taylor for her healing prayers. Richard Price. Dr. Natalie Coburn and her team. As well as Dr. Paula Fishman.

And, finally, a special thank you to my wife, Renée, for her enduring love and her relentless caring support and devotion during a recent health crisis. I am eternally grateful. My love for you increases each second.